Magdalen Nabb was born in Lancashire in 1917 and trained as a potter. In 1975 she abandoned pottery, sold her home and her car, and went to Florence with her son, knowing nobody and speaking no Italian. She has lived there ever since, and pursues a dual career as crime writer and – with the immensely successful Josie Smith books – children's author.

She has written ten crime novels featuring Marshal Guarnaccia of the carabinieri, all set in Florence, which she describes as 'a very secret city. Walk down any residential street and you have no idea what is going on behind those blank walls. It's a problem the Marshal comes up against all the time.'

MAGDALEN NABB

The Marshal at the Villa Torrini

HarperCollins*Publishers*

HarperCollins*Publishers*
77–85 Fulham Palace Road,
Hammersmith, London W6 8JB

This paperback edition 1997
1 3 5 7 9 8 6 4 2

First published in Great Britain by
HarperCollins*Publishers* 1993

Copyright © Magdalen Nabb 1993

The Author asserts the moral right to
be identified as the author of this work

ISBN 0 00 647891 3

Set in Baskerville

Printed and bound in Great Britain by
Caledonian International Book Manufacturing Ltd, Glasgow

Although this story is set very specifically in Florence and its environs, all the characters and events in it are entirely fictitious and no resemblance is intended to any real person, either living or dead.

CHAPTER 1

'I suppose I might have pushed her.'

'You *suppose* you might have pushed her?' The Public Prosecutor's voice rose on the last word and then he paused. A nervous cough echoed round the high courtroom as though between movements at a concert. The silence stretched out. Sweat began to gleam on the prisoner's bony forehead. The Prosecutor whisked back the black silk wings of his gown and attacked.

'Did you or did you not push her?'

'I did! I did push her, I suppose . . .'

'And do you also suppose that you pushed her hard enough to knock her to the floor?'

He was such a puny creature it was difficult to imagine him knocking anybody down. His pale limp hair was greasy and his clothes looked too big, like hand-me-downs, though it was likely he'd lost weight in prison. He was in his thirties, but the thin shoulders and vacant, bruised-looking eyes gave him the look of a half-starved, battered child. His knees and hands were pressed together as though he needed to work at keeping his balance on the isolated plastic chair. He was shaking, though, so perhaps that was what he was fighting against. Not from guilt, not from the memory of that night. He was only afraid of what was happening to him.

'She did fall . . .' His eyes strayed to the cages on the left where a more robust prisoner wept silently into his hands, his body rocking slightly.

'Please answer the question!'

'She . . .' He dragged his gaze away from the cage but it was clear that he didn't remember what the question was. 'She did fall . . . She was drunk, though.'

'She was drunk.' The Prosecutor's habit of repeating everything he said would have unnerved the most innocent witness, but this man was beyond the reach of such pin-pricks. Again his eyes swivelled to the cage. Only half his attention was on the Prosecutor's questions.

'So: she was drunk, you pushed her and she fell. Is that all?'

An incomprehensible mumble.

'Please speak up so that the court can hear your answers!'

'She might have banged into something.'

'Banged into something? A wall? A floor? A piece of furni-ture? What might she have banged into?'

'There was a chest of drawers in the entrance near where she fell.'

The sobs of the prisoner in the cage now became audible throughout the courtroom. This evidently didn't displease the Prosecutor since it provided suitable sound effects for his climax.

'And so, Your Honour, ladies and gentlemen of the jury, Anna Maria Grazzini, aged thirty-five and in robust health, after receiving "a bit of a push" and falling near a chest of drawers—was found dead on arrival at the hospital of Santa Maria Nuova from injuries which included a frac-tured jaw and cranium, five broken ribs and a punctured pancreas! She must have fallen very *awkwardly*, wouldn't you say, Signor Pecchioli?'

It was well-judged. The background sobbing noise had risen as his voice rose, describing the horror of that Christ-mas Eve.

'Your Honour, I would like the photographs of Anna Maria Grazzini to be shown to the jury.'

One by one they looked at the photographs and you could see their eyes glazing over in the hope of duti-fully looking without actually seeing. All of them then looked at the puny creature on the plastic chair more intently.

The Prosecutor knew his business all right but it was so unnecessary. Pecchioli had no hope of saving himself. He was only waiting for it to be over, to get back to the safety of his cell, eat something, have a smoke. The photos had provided cover for some serious coughing and nose-blowing. At least half the people in court must have been at some stage of the influenza which an unnaturally warm February had helped to spread throughout Florence. The photographs were removed.

The defence was trying for manslaughter for all three accused but given what had happened afterwards there was no real hope. Pecchioli's lawyer probably had his thoughts, too, on lunch and a good bottle of wine. He wasn't even looking at the Prosecutor who was on his feet and proceeding.

'Did you hit Anna Maria Grazzini after she fell near the chest of drawers?'

'No. I never hit her. No.'

'Then how do you account for the injuries I've just described? I take it that you can account for them? You were there. You pushed her, you *suppose*. At any rate, she fell. What happened next?'

'I tried . . .' His voice failed and he coughed, then stopped. The small hand with chewed nails reached out towards the microphone without quite touching it, as though that might be the cause.

'I—she was drunk. I tried to make her get up.'

'How? Did you kick her?'

'I might have prodded her a bit with my foot, like you would.'

'Prodded her.'

'We all did. She was drunk. She wouldn't get up.'

'We'll come to what you all did in a moment. Where

exactly did you, as you put it, prod her? Or would it be
more precise to say kicked her? More, as it might be, con-
comitant with the nature, extent and gravity of the resulting
injuries?'

'I don't know what you mean.'

'In what sense do you not know what I mean? Are you
suggesting—'

'It's the words you're using. They're too long. I don't
know what you're saying.'

For a moment the Prosecutor was nonplussed and it was
written all over his face just how mortified he was that a
little runt like that had dared to interrupt him mid-sentence
and criticize his language. He soon recovered and started
speaking slowly and clearly as though to a foreigner.

'Did *you* . . . kick . . . Anna Maria Grazzini *after* you had
pushed her so that she *fell*.'

'I probably . . .' His voice failed again and you could see
his Adam's apple working as he swallowed repeatedly. 'I
can't remember. I was pissed off with her because it was
Christmas. Because of the kid. I probably kicked her a bit,
we all did. She wouldn't get up.'

'Whose idea was it to do what you did next? Yours?'

'I don't know. We were all in a state. It was all of us
. . . I don't know . . .'

'Who made the first telephone call?'

'Chiara . . . She called the police.'

'Chiara Giorgetti?'

'Yes.'

'And was this call made from the flat?'

'No. They went to a call-box.'

'And you remained behind?'

'Somebody had to stay with the kid. There were two of
them so they could manage . . . they could manage to . . .'

The Prosecutor made no comment. The jury knew what
they had managed to do, they'd already heard the evidence

of Mario Saverino whose sobs had now turned to rhythmic groans. He had cried throughout his cross-examination.

Having given the jury a moment to consider what had been 'managed', the Prosecutor continued.

'However, you do know the outcome of that call to the police because Chiara Giorgetti and Mario Saverino then telephoned you, did they not?'

'Yes.'

'To tell you what?'

'The police wouldn't come. They said it was none of their business and to call an ambulance.'

'And did they call an ambulance?'

'No. They told me they were going to the Palazzo Pitti and that I should wait ten minutes and then call there.'

'Which you did?'

'Yes.'

'You waited, I take it, the full ten minutes?'

'Yes.'

This, too, was allowed to sink in before the next question was put with an almost casual air.

'Tell me, when you last saw Anna Maria Grazzini, was she conscious?'

Pecchioli took a long time to consider this but couldn't produce an answer.

'Could she speak?' prompted the Prosecutor.

'Nothing you could understand.' And again he insisted, 'She was drunk.'

'There was a great deal more than that wrong with her at the time we're speaking of! Did she attempt to speak or make any noise of any kind?'

'She was making a noise . . . noises . . . short grunting noises, like a dog when it's going to be sick.'

'No further questions.' The Prosecutor adjusted his gown and was seated.

The judge looked up, his face expressionless.

'Defence?'

'No questions.'

The judge looked around him. 'Did I understand that we're not to hear the pathologist's evidence until tomorrow for some reason?'

The Prosecutor shot to his feet. 'That is correct, Your Honour, he—'

'Very well. Call your next witness, please.'

'Call Salvatore Guarnaccia, Marshal-in-Chief of the Carabinieri, in command of the Pitti Palace Station.'

The Marshal had been sitting through all this with his big hands planted on his knees, his huge eyes almost unblinking, his forehead creased in concentration. Filled with apprehension, he now got slowly to his feet.

'Salva? Is that you? How did it go?'

'It didn't.' He placed his hat on the hall table and went straight into the bedroom to change out of uniform. Usually he wandered into the kitchen first to say Hello and see what was for lunch. Teresa registered this symptom of ill-temper and salted the water which had just come to the boil. When he did appear she was tearing open a fresh packet of spaghetti.

'How do you mean, it didn't go? Do you want pasta or not?'

'No. Yes. Just a bit. Or I could just have salad.'

'You can't live on salad—for goodness' sake, Salva, you ate three pieces of chocolate cake last night and now it's salad. Your liver doesn't know whether it's coming or going and neither do I. Why can't you eat sensibly? I'll be glad when the boys get back and we've done with this whole business.'

The idea, the Marshal's not his wife's, was that while the two children were away skiing on their school trip he should take the opportunity to detoxify his liver. The process involved days of picking morosely at bowls of salad, punctuated by episodes like the chocolate cake which he had consumed in equally morose silence, fixing every forkful with a gaze so filled with sorrow and resentment that it might have been the cake eating him.

Teresa shot the pasta into the water and give it a brisk stir.

'I've put a bit in for you. The most sensible thing to do is to eat a half portion of pasta without the sauce and don't drink any wine. Then a bit of salad.'

There was no denying the truth of this. There was also no denying that a dish of white spaghetti accompanied by a glass of water would depress the most cheerful of spirits.

'It'll be five or six minutes.'

The Marshal stumped off to the sitting-room and switched on the television news. Her voice followed him.

'If we'd taken them skiing ourselves you could have done some walking, got some fresh air and exercise and really done something for your health, never mind picking at salads. And what's more it wouldn't have cost half of what we've paid out for two of them if we'd stayed at the military skiing club, but it's like talking to a wall . . .'

The news on channel two was finishing and the Marshal switched to channel one.

'I wouldn't care if you'd anything concrete to say against it!'

That was true. The Marshal rarely offered arguments. He either did things or remained inert. He didn't like mountains.

'Mohammed!' With this finale the contents of the pan sloshed into the colander and the Marshal, hearing it, got to his feet.

He lingered a moment to watch two more politicians being led off in handcuffs, then switched off.

'Country's ruled by bandits,' he announced, reappearing in the kitchen.

'Mind out of my way. You will plant yourself in the middle of the kitchen like a road block when I'm cooking . . . Have I put the bread out? I haven't . . . Salva, I need to get to the cupboard . . .' The protest was automatic and rhetorical. In fifteen years of marriage she had lost hope of curing him of this habit of fetching up like a beached whale wherever the action was. The rest of the family just had to flow round him as they might a cumbersome piece of furniture.

Once they were at table she took a closer look at him and said, 'You're hungry, that's what's the matter with you.'

'I've wasted my whole morning, that's what's the matter.'

'What? Because you had to go to court?'

'Because I was there for hours and when they got to me the defence suddenly asked for an adjournment. Some problem over the child's evidence and whether she should be made to testify against her own mother.'

'Well, I'm not surprised. I only know what I read in the papers, of course . . .' Another piece of habitual rhetoric. He never told her anything, or so she said. 'Still, I'd say that child had been through enough without having to appear in court. Having to sit there in front of all those people and answer questions, imagine . . .'

The Marshal, who had been imagining nothing else for the last few days, said crossly, 'I can't eat this without even a drop of oil—it's all sticking together!'

Teresa gave him a brief trickle of oil and a teaspoonful of grated cheese. 'You're not still worrying yourself over this new system, are you? It's the same for everyone, you know, Salva. I'm sure even the judges and lawyers won't be finding it easy, either.'

'Judges and lawyers have university degrees. And besides, I'm too old.'

'Old? What d'you mean, old?'

'I mean too old to be studying. That sort of thing's all very well when you're twenty—not that I was any good at it then . . .' He glowered sideways at the glass of water that should have been wine.

'You might as well give me your plate. That pasta's stone cold by now. Have some salad. Anyway, it's not as though you've never been in court before.'

'Hmph. Giving my name and rank and confirming that my written report was accurate. Thank you and goodbye.'

'For heaven's sake, Salva, anybody would think you were on trial yourself. There's no reason why you should be frightened of being cross-examined.'

'How do you know about being cross-examined?'

'I watch Perry Mason. You sleep through it.'

'Hmph.'

She started clearing away. 'I'll put the coffee on. Why don't you have a pear, they're lovely. It's raining again! What a miserable day.' She switched the light on and filled the coffee pot.

He peeled the pear slowly. Was it worth going through the copy of his report yet again this evening? He wasn't even sure now when he would be called. He'd tried to learn the thing by heart, especially the dates and times and so on. It was only too easy to imagine himself with a mental block in the face of some clever lawyer who might try to confuse him or somehow trip him up. Make him look a fool, at the very least. Grim memories of oral exams at school surfaced to make him cringe with embarrassment after all those years. At least now they couldn't rap his knuckles with a ruler or make him kneel in the corner on grains of rice. Only times he'd been grateful for his plumpness as a lad. His poor little mate, Vittorio, in his oversized hand-me-down clothes had the boniest knees in the class, and he was constantly in trouble. The nuns must have known his mother was a prostitute and they were always hard on him. His knees never got time to heal before Sister Benedetta had him back in the corner kneeling on the rice again.

'Do you want a drop of milk in it?'

'Sister Benedetta was tougher than any assize court judge.'

'Salva!'

'What?'

'I'm asking you if you want milk. What are you rambling on about?'

'Just a drop. Nuns. I was thinking about nuns . . .'

'Oh . . . Oh—I meant to tell you, there's a good film on TV tonight.'

'I thought I'd go through the file on this new criminal procedure again, just in case . . .'

'Not again! Go to sleep over it, you mean. You know you can never keep your eyes open after supper. You've slept with that file on your chest for I don't know how many evenings together. You've fallen asleep holding the thing in bed. You might as well fall asleep in front of a good film.'

And the Marshal, fed up to the teeth of the whole business, had half a mind to do just that. But he never got the chance, because before he even got to eat his supper, perhaps at the very moment when he was signing the daily orders for tomorrow and thinking of forgetting the court case and the diet for tonight, the Signora Eugenia Torrini decided she should call the carabinieri no matter *what* Giorgio said.

'Let's hope this is it.'

They were on the side of the hill behind the Belvedere

fort and twice already the Marshal's driver had lost his
way in the dark and attempted driveways that turned out
to be the wrong ones. Then he'd had to back out precariously on to the narrow, winding Via San Leonardo. This
time they had better luck. A longer drive lined by the silhouettes of cypress trees which turned out, as the caller
had explained, to be not really a driveway at all but a
rutted country lane running past the side of the Villa Torrini. Their headlights picked out a gate on the left.

'Can't see any lights . . .'

The driver pulled up and opened his door to shine a
torch on the gate. It was a large wooden gate, painted
green, with a brass plaque saying TORRINI. It was padlocked
and gleamed with drops of rain in the torchlight.

They drove on and turned in behind the house, stopping
the car on a wet dirt track. There were lights showing here.
Two windows of the villa and one small window in what
looked like a converted barn a few yards away. It was one
of the odd things about Florence which the Marshal had
always liked, the way the city could often end abruptly and
you were in the country.

'You can wait for me here.'

A faint drizzle touched his face as he got out, and the
night air smelled of rotten leaves and wet grass. It was very
quiet and the Marshal's footsteps were loud on the paved
court in front of the door. Ghostly lemon or orange trees
in huge pots were shrouded in polythene on each side. He
pressed the lighted doorbell but he could already hear
heavy bolts being drawn inside. She was bound to have
heard his arrival. A rattle of keys. Then a pause, perhaps
for second thoughts, before a low-pitched woman's voice
asked, 'Who is it?'

'Carabinieri, Signora. You called us.'

'Oh dear . . .' More rattling keys. 'I'm so sorry, you'll
have to wait a minute. I can't find the other keys.'

He heard her walk away from the door, with a stick if he wasn't mistaken. She was still murmuring to herself in distress, 'Oh dear . . . Giorgio's right, I get worse . . . Oh, where can I have . . .'

Good job it wasn't cold. Some sort of creeper was growing all over this side of the house. That's how you knew this wasn't the real country, you could see too well at night. The sky wasn't properly dark because of the city nearby. Out in the real country, if there wasn't a fullish moon, you couldn't see your hand in front of your face but you could see stars, millions of them. She was coming back . . . More keys.

'Ooh . . . ! I'm so sorry. This is what getting old means . . .'

She was still undoing a series of locks. Eight turns each!

At last the door opened and a tall, dignified woman looked out at him. 'Oooh, I am sorry, I really am. I always intend to put them in the same place so I can find them but something always happens. The telephone rings or something and I go off with them in my hand and there we are. You will forgive me?' She looked at him anxiously.

'Of course. We all do these things . . .'

He expected to step inside on this line but though she did open the door a little wider he was left where he was. She was dressed very neatly, all in grey.

'Giorgio's right, I should be more organized about things. The older you get, the more important it is. You can't improvise, you know, at my age. I don't know what you must think . . . Do forgive me.'

A second absolution accompanied by a slight forward movement at last gained him entrance and she apologized for keeping him on the doorstep.

'Giorgio's always telling me, and he's right, he says "Stop talking just every so often and think what you're doing," but of course I forget—then, you know, living alone . . .'

He followed her into a long room divided into dining-
and sitting-room by an archway. Without looking round
much he was aware of pale colours, soft carpets under his
feet, great comfort and solid wealth. He was also aware of
a great deal of smoke.

'Do sit down and I'll explain everything and then you
can decide what to do—if you don't think I'm just being
a foolish old woman. I always sit here, you can see . . .'

The corner of a large pale sofa. A little stack of paperback
books was balanced on the arm, and cigarettes, a gold
lighter and a glass with a bottle of whisky were on the low
table drawn up before it. The Marshal took the armchair
opposite her, settled his hat on his knee and waited. He
knew from experience that you had to let people tell things
in their own way and their own time and if it turned out
that she was simply lonely and fearful and in need of
reassurance, then so be it. The only trouble was that the
rumblings of his neglected stomach must be audible.

'You've a lot of books,' he remarked loudly to cover one
particularly noisy protest. The wall behind her was covered
in them, floor to ceiling.

'Oh yes, I read all day. The trouble is I smoke all day,
as well. Can I offer you . . . ?'

'No . . . No, I don't, thank you.'

'I shouldn't myself, Giorgio's always telling me . . . But
there aren't many vices open to me at my age so I enjoy
my cigarettes and a glass or two of whisky in the evening.
If you'd like some, perhaps you'd get yourself a glass. That
cupboard there.'

'No, no. Thank you.' He had never touched the stuff in
his life.

'It takes me so long to get up with this wretched stick.
Oh, it's a bad business getting old. You don't feel any
different inside—I don't, anyway—so it's like being imprisoned in a body you hardly recognize as your own. I

wouldn't mind dying. I'm serious. I can't enjoy myself and I'm neither use nor ornament to anybody else. That's why I enjoy Celia's company. She makes me feel I am useful. Giorgio says she's just being kind but even so. We exchange books—she writes, you see and she reads as much as I do and I love to read English novels. Now, tell me the truth, how many people can you lend books to and know they'll come back? Can you name one friend?'

'Well, I don't . . .'

'You see? Are you sure you won't?' She lit a fresh cigarette. 'Celia's the only one—you can understand it of course, her being a writer. These are for her.' She tapped the pile on the arm of the sofa.

The Marshal watched her, waiting. He wasn't really following her discourse about books. It was one of the things that annoyed his wife, that he got left behind when people were telling him things. He was still thinking, now, of this woman imprisoned in her own body. Her grey hair was nicely waved, her eyes deep blue. You could see she had always been very good-looking. She wore no make-up or jewellery.

'So you tell me. What do you think we should do? I know Giorgio would say I'm being neurotic but he's away and he won't find out until he telephones me at his usual time tomorrow. He was furious about me calling the priest.'

The Marshal, caught out, tried to cover his inattention. 'You thought a priest was needed as well as—'

'A priest! Not in this house. No priest sets foot in here unless I lose my wits completely. I've seen too many of my women friends fall into the hands of the priests and I told Giorgio, I said, it isn't as though they were after anything other than your money—might be more interesting! What do you think? Anyway, I don't want you to feel I'm hurrying you, but don't you think we should do something? I've tried telephoning five or six times—Giorgio would say

I'm being a nuisance and they don't want to be disturbed, but you can't know who it is until you pick the phone up, can you? And you see how I'm handicapped. I did think of going and knocking on their door but in the dark I'd probably fall. All I want you to do is go and look, try and make them hear. They are there, you know. Their car's parked there and there's a light on. If you look out that window you'll see it.'

The Marshal got to his feet and went to look out at the darkness. He made out the paved court he had crossed, his car and driver and the lighted window of the converted barn.

'Who are these people and when did you last see them?' He was still looking out.

'Celia, I told you. Celia and her husband Julian. They're in there. I saw them come home together with some shopping about half past five. I went to the door—I wasn't being nosey, I would never do that, but she'd brought me some fresh milk. We fixed to have a drink together and exchange some books between about six and half past— well, it's nearly nine o'clock and they don't answer the phone! Oh, I'm being a foolish old woman, aren't I?'

The Marshal really didn't know.

'Which light is it that's on?'

'The bathroom light. I saw it on when I closed my shutters and I thought: There's Celia having her bath—she likes a long lazy bath with a glass of something beside her. Even so, when she hadn't turned up by a quarter to seven I opened the shutters and looked—well, you don't stay in the bath for over an hour and so I started phoning. You can't say it isn't odd.'

In the Marshal's experience people were odd but he didn't say so. He did say, more to calm her anxiety than anything, 'It's possible they've fallen asleep, left the light on.'

'I know what you really mean.' As she said this he turned to look at her, surprised. 'But there hasn't been anything like that between them for some time. Celia tells me things and I listen to her. Whatever Giorgio says, it can be a help when someone listens.'

'Yes. Yes, it can.'

'You see, I'm so afraid of wasting your time, but I'd never forgive myself if something turned out to be wrong and I—'

'Don't worry, Signora. You did quite right. Just sit here quietly and finish your drink while I go over there and see if I can make myself heard.'

'Wait . . .' She struggled to her feet. 'There are keys to the barn somewhere . . . Celia always says if there's an emergency or even should she lose her keys, you know, and I'm sure I can lay my hands on them . . .'

It took, as expected, some time.

The Marshal accepted the keys, forgave her, and stepped outside.

The driver, seeing him, started up the engine.

'No, no . . . Come with me. Something wrong in the barn there.

Though he hadn't said so until now, he was just as sure there was something wrong as the Signora Torrini was. It was too quiet, for a start. In a place like this you should hear someone turning the page of a book, at least the odd remark spoken from room to room. And then, that bathroom window. He didn't like that bathroom window. It was lit up but it wasn't steamed up. Nothing you could quite put your finger on.

'Ring the bell.'

After two or three rings they looked at each other. The driver, a wide-eyed young recruit from Sardinia by the name of Giuseppe Fara, said, 'Shall I break the door down, Marshal?'

The Marshal took out the key from his pocket and opened the door.

Once inside, he pounded on the inner surface of the door and shouted, 'Carabinieri! Anyone there?'

There was no answer.

'See if you can find a light switch.'

After some fumbling about, Fara found one. It was a pretty room, square and colourful with a terracotta floor. One side was set up as a kitchen, the other had bright rugs and wicker armchairs. A giant pot held bulrushes and tall feathery stuff. There was a big country-style fireplace, brought there, no doubt, from some peasant's cottage. The Marshal approached it. The logs had settled into the wood ash but they still glowed faintly. The room was warm.

'Should we go upstairs, Marshal?' Fara indicated the spiral wood and iron staircase in the corner.

'You wait here.' He saw both disappointment and relief on the lad's face as he began his climb. The staircase wasn't built for someone of his bulk and he went slowly. Upstairs, the square space had been divided into a small bathroom on the left, the light on and the door ajar, and a bedroom to the right. That door, too, was slightly ajar but the room was in darkness. The Marshal pushed open the bathroom door.

There was no steam. The room was cold, the red water cool with a pinkish foam on it. The room didn't smell of death but of a flowery perfume, the bath foam, presumably. The woman in the bath was dead, her head lolling towards the Marshal, half way into the water. He couldn't see, of course, with the water so clouded with blood, but it looked like a standard sort of suicide, wrists cut in the bath. It wasn't his business to go any further so he descended the spiral staircase carefully.

'Woman's dead in the bath,' he said to the boy's inquiring look. 'Can you see a phone?'

'On that little table by the fireplace.'

He phoned the magistrate on duty and then Headquarters at Borgo Ognissanti for technicians and a photographer. Then he started wandering about the room, his large, slightly bulging eyes taking everything in. Young Fara watched him, not wanting to show his ignorance by asking what they were looking for. If he had, the Marshal couldn't have told him. He just stared at everything, his mind elsewhere.

At one point he remarked loudly, 'Where the devil's the husband taken himself to, anyway?'

'Did you check the bedroom . . .' The lad tailed off, thinking he was out of line saying it, but then there was a loud bump directly above their heads. It startled both of them and the lad's face paled. It was really to cover his terror that he dashed up the spiral staircase first. The Marshal, understanding, followed, only murmuring, 'Be careful, don't go in.'

The lad obeyed. He pushed the door with one finger and found the light switch. The two of them stood there staring in silence. They saw what had made the noise, a Chianti flask thudding to the floor. It was leaking its last red drops on to a white goatskin rug.

'Is he dead, d'you think . . . ?'

The Marshal strode forward and turned the bearded face up. It flopped back on the counterpane when he let it go.

'No,' he said, 'he's not. He's drunk. Very drunk.'

CHAPTER 2

'If you've taken your samples can we let the bath water out?' It was a doctor the Marshal had never met before and he was doing his best not to be in his way, conscious of his bulk in the small bathroom.

The red water gurgled slowly away, spluttering and choking as it went. The doctor carefully lifted one of the woman's feet, the heel of which was blocking the plughole. 'Otherwise we'll be here all night. Photo?'

The photographer's flash got busy as the body appeared out of the water. Then it stopped and they looked at each other.

'Well, that's a turn-up . . .' The doctor picked up one wrist and then the other. Not a mark. 'Not so much as a scratch. Well, all that blood came from somewhere. Can we turn her? Got all your photos?'

'Fine by me.'

'Marshal?'

The Marshal had taken all the notes he needed before they arrived. He nodded.

The three of them turned her over.

'Ah. Well, not what you'd expect, of course, but explains the bleeding at any rate.'

A wine glass lay broken under the body and had made two very deep cuts in one buttock and a number of scratches on the lower back. One triangle of glass was still deeply embedded in the wound it had made.

'That's not our cause of death. I wonder . . .'

The Marshal, too, was wondering. Sometimes people fainted in the bath, though he'd never come across such a thing himself—anyway weren't they usually old people? It was one thing to faint, but when you felt yourself drowning wouldn't you come to? Start to struggle? Somebody feeble might not save themselves in time but this woman . . .

'How old do you think she is, Doctor?'

'Forty-five-ish, I should think. I'll take her temperature now I've got her turned over. Time of death likely to be a problem for you?'

'No. No . . . She was seen earlier and then the husband . . .'

Considerable noise was coming from the bedroom where young Fara was battling to bring the drunken man to his senses without much success.

'Could have been drunk like him, I suppose . . .'

'Well, I can't give you an official opinion on that at this stage, but I doubt it.'

'Hmph.'

'Probably an accident.'

Fara's now desperate voice was eliciting nothing more than faint groans next door.

'I'll bring him round for you,' the doctor said, 'as soon as I've finished here.'

The Marshal took to wandering about the house again, though his wanderings were not as random now as before. He looked, not very wholeheartedly, for a suicide note. He found a desk whose top right-hand drawer contained the passports of Celia Rose Carter, born in Great Britain in 1947 and Julian Forbes, also British, born in 1959. He frowned and opened the woman's passport again.

'Eh, Marshal? What do you think?'

He realized that the technicians who were packing up their equipment at the kitchen end of the room had been talking to him and he hadn't heard a word. He looked at them blankly. 'I'm sorry. Wasn't listening.'

'It was nothing. Find anything interesting?'

The Marshal looked down at the passport again but all he said was, 'It's her birthday . . .'

'Don't worry about me, I'm fine.' Julian Forbes rolled back on to his stomach and added carefully, 'Just tell people I've fallen asleep on one of the beds.' Once again he was sleeping like a baby. Fara looked at the Marshal for help but the Marshal was no expert.

'We might have to let him sleep it off . . .'

The doctor came in, drying his hands on a linen towel.

'Let's get miladdo awake, then.' He approached the bed and turned Forbes on his back. With the rather hairy back of his still damp hand he rubbed Forbes's mouth and nose briskly. Forbes opened his eyes and at once the doctor swung him upright. The drunken flush on the cheeks drained away.

'Going to be sick . . .'

'Be my guest.' The doctor tipped some dried flowers out of a jar on the floor and Forbes vomited a good litre of red wine into it. Passing the jar to Fara, the doctor suggested, 'See if the technicians want a sample of that—and make some coffee while you're down there. He's all yours, Marshal.'

The doctor returned to the bathroom to clean the splashes of vomit from himself. The Marshal stood beside the bed, looking down. Young as Forbes was, he was losing the hair on his crown. The hands held to the temples, no doubt in the hope of containing a headache, were long-fingered and pale.

'Christ, I feel terrible! What's happened? Not a road accident—I never drive. Celia always drives . . .'

'You get drunk very often?'

'No, I don't.' His voice was peevish. 'It just affects me badly sometimes, that's all. Now what the hell's going on? Who are all these people?'

'If you can get as far as the bathroom—'

The word acted on him like a knife in the stomach. He double forward with a wail of panic and then curled sideways on the bed and began to sob in a high-pitched voice like a child.

The Marshal sighed inwardly. It was going to be a long night. A commotion outside announced the arrival of the magistrate. The Marshal's relief turned to dismay, however, when the magistrate's head appeared round the door, his eyes bright with irony, a small cigar in his mouth.

'They said it was you. Splendid! What have we got— apart from an appalling smell of vomit?' He held out his hand, giving a wicked smirk in the direction of the sobbing figure.

The Marshal shook hands.

'His wife . . .' He nodded towards the bathroom and the magistrate popped across to look.

Forbes, without ceasing to cry, asked, 'Who's that, for God's sake?'

'Substitute Prosecutor Fusarri.' And if the Marshal, too, was thinking, 'For God's sake,' he didn't say it aloud.

Fusarri wandered back in, cigar poised delicately aloft. He never spilled a flake of ash on his fine grey suits. Forbes was still sobbing loudly, his face covered by his hands.

'What's his name?' mouthed Fusarri silently.

The Marshal offered his notebook.

'Well, well, Mr Forbes. What have you been doing to your wife?'

Now that was the trouble with Fusarri. He had no scruples, no tact! The Marshal who had been thinking precisely the same thing would never have dreamt of saying it. He was Milanese, of course, so you couldn't expect . . . Even so, he always left the Marshal uncomfortable. He never knew whether the chap was serious or not. Not, to look at his face, but then you couldn't be sure . . . One thing was sure, he knew how to sort this Forbes character to whom the Marshal had already taken a strong dislike. It was a pleasure to watch.

'Your wife is dead, sir, and in what look to us to be unusual circumstances. It may, of course, have been an accident, in which case we shall have no need to bother you further once we have the results of the post-mortem. In the meantime we require the answers to a few questions.'

Forbes still had his head in his hands, but he'd quietened down. Fusarri sat neatly down beside him and a curl of pungent cigar smoke found its way from the smiling mouth in the direction of Forbes's eyes. He lifted his head to cough.

'Good, good. I see we understand each other. So much more comfortable here than in somebody's office, don't you think?'

'Well, Marshal.' Fusarri stood up and strode out of the room, waving the little cigar at shoulder height. 'He's all yours!'

The Marshal stood there, staring down. He certainly wasn't going to sit on the bed for a start. Fusarri . . . The Marshal had no vocabulary to deal with Fusarri. It was the standard complaint that the magistrates trod all over the police and carabinieri, armchair detectives most of them, giving out orders like generals who never go near the battlefield. But Fusarri . . .

'Hmph.'

The Marshal fetched himself a wickerwork chair, hoped it was up to his weight, and sat down near Forbes.

'Tell me about it,' he said.

Forbes crossed one leg tightly over the other and folded his arms. His forehead and nose became beaded with sweat. He smelled of alcohol, of vomit and of fear. He didn't look at the Marshal and he didn't say a word.

'You'll have to, you know. Me or somebody else.'

Forbes darted a quick glance at the Marshal and then

his eyes swivelled away. He was sweating so profusely now that some drops rolled down his temples and down under his open shirt collar which was striped green and white. Since there was nothing to listen to, the Marshal's big eyes looked, taking in every detail. A brown sweater that looked very old—it was certainly very worn. The striped shirt stuck out through the elbows and a bit of unravelled wool was hanging . . . Corduroy trousers, rather baggy, red wool socks. He was thin, but there were signs of an incipient pot belly. Too much drink, probably.

The Marshal was prepared to sit in silence for as long as was necessary. If you keep on asking questions people go on refusing to answer, but silence is very unnerving and a nervous person will try to fill it, no matter how reluctant he is to tell you anything. This man was nervous all right. So the Marshal, hands planted firmly on his knees, eyes fixed on his prey, waited.

Forbes was shaking now and having difficulty staying still, so that the Marshal knew what he wanted to do was get up and run and keep running. The reaction of a frightened animal. And yet he was surely an intelligent man. The Signora Torrini hadn't said much about him, come to think of it, she'd only talked about the woman. A writer . . . Well, she wouldn't be married to a road-sweeper, he didn't suppose. Besides, his hands . . . He'd never done a stroke of physical work in his life.

One of the slim-fingered hands now fished in a trouser pocket. Forbes pulled out a handkerchief and dried his brow thoroughly. It immediately became beaded with drops again. He went on mopping himself. It was something to fill the vacuum but it wasn't enough. He said, 'I can't remember anything. It happens when I drink.' He bent over and righted the Chianti flask that had rolled from the bed on to the rug. To hide his face, the Marshal thought.

'I understand. Perhaps you'd like to go to the bathroom and clean yourself up.'

He went rigid. 'Is she . . . have you . . .'

'She's still there,' the Marshal said. 'But I thought you didn't remember. The bathroom seemed to ring a bell last time I mentioned it.'

A pause. His mind was going like a steam engine, you could almost hear it. He was intelligent all right, but they were the ones who in the end always talked themselves into trouble. The stout denial of the most stupid criminal was much more effective, but a chap like this one couldn't keep it up. The temptation to run rings round a bunch of none-too-bright policemen was always too great, and sooner or later the brilliant story that explained everything would be concocted. Still Forbes was being cautious—or the hang-over was saving him.

'I remembered when you said it. That . . .'

The Marshal didn't help him. He sat very still and hardly appeared to be interested even. His ear was cocked to Fusarri's fast rattling accent with its slurred Milanese S. He would have filled the entire house by this time with the pungent blue smoke of his tiny cigars which he chain-smoked. He'd be sure to get on well with Signora Torrini. A vehicle drew up outside. Doors slammed and someone gave an order.

The Marshal sighed and his heavy, black uniformed torso made an almost imperceptible movement forward. The other man flinched and drew back.

'That will be the ambulance. Do you want to see your wife before they take her away?'

Forbes dried his brow quickly and swallowed hard.

'What's happened to her?'

It was so calculated, so infantile, so blatantly false that the Marshal, thinking of a still young woman lying dead and alone for hours while he snored in a drunken stupor, could have hit him. Someone else in his place might have done just that and perhaps saved himself a lot of time and trouble since the man was clearly a moral and physical coward. But the Marshal didn't move.

'I don't know,' he said, and waited.

But Forbes only narrowed his eyes and then dropped his head once again into his hands.

'Oh God . . . My head!'

It was useless. The headache and nausea were more pressing than any need to save himself from accusation. Besides which, it could well turn out after the autopsy that there was nothing to accuse him of. After all, there was no getting away from the fact that he had been found asleep next door to his dead wife when he had a car and a current passport at his disposal. At any rate, it was useless to try and do much with him until he recovered. The Marshal got to his feet and again Forbes made that slight cring- ing movement which he covered by opening the bedside cabinet.

'Christ almighty, I need some aspirin . . .'

There were a few boxes of pills in the cupboard.

'If your wife was in the habit of taking sleeping pills or tranquillizers of any sort I'll need to take them with me.'

Forbes swept everything out of the cupboard on to the floor in a fury. 'Shit!'

'In the bathroom, are they?'

The man flung himself back against the crumpled pillows and started weeping loudly again.

'Did she?' insisted the Marshal.

'Did she what? Oh God! Oh God . . .'

'Take sleeping pills?' But what was the use? The Marshal stooped and picked up the tablets, checking each label. Mineral salts, throat pastilles, a tube of liniment for sprains and bruises, capsules for relief from colds. Nothing. He put them back and closed the cabinet door. As he stood up he noticed a little screw of paper in a flowered ashtray by the bedside lamp. Picking it up, he gave a sideways glance at the sobbing figure on the bed. Forbes again had his hands over his face and was burrowing into the pillows as though he hoped they might envelop him completely. The Marshal unscrewed the twist of paper. There were two red capsules in it.

'Are these sleeping pills?'

Forbes didn't even look up.

'Oh God, my head . . .'

'I'll need to take them away. You'll be given a receipt.'

Fusarri's voice called from the bathroom. By the sound of it, they were starting to remove the body.

'Are you sure you don't wish to see your wife before they take her away?'

His only response was to curl in on himself, drawing up his knees in a fœtal position. The Marshal stood staring down at him. He must still be drunk, of course, but even so . . .

'Marshal!'

'Yes, sir.'

It was no easy business for the porters to get their burden down the spiral staircase. They had to keep it vertical and they were afraid of slipping and breaking their necks. They complained bitterly.

'Go more slowly, for God's sake, or there'll be three stiffs to shift instead of one.'

'Keep your voice down. I think the husband's up there . . .'

'Doing what? Powdering his nose?'

'They might well ask,' the Marshal said as the porters reached the floor below and he and the Prosecutor followed.

Fusarri began wandering about the living-room, his little cigar held aloft.

'Find a suicide note?'

'No, sir.'

'Didn't expect to, either, did you?' Fusarri paused in his wanderings and fixed the Marshal with a bright glance.

'No, sir.'

'Ah. Well, of course, I'm no expert . . .' He wandered on.

He always made some remark like that, but what the devil did he mean by it? That he really was an expert—he was supposed to be an expert, damn it, that was his job . . . or did he really mean, 'Don't imagine *you're* an expert'? Now he was flipping open their passports as the Marshal had done earlier, the cigar parked at the side of his mouth and his eyes half closed against the smoke.

'So what did you find?'

'Her date of birth on the passport . . .'

'Which tells you.'

'It's her birthday today.'

'Ha!'

'And he's a lot younger. I also found these.'

'Sleeping pills, d'you think?'

'Possibly.'

'Find out. Then send them over to me. And I think we'll hang on to that young man's passport for the moment. See to the receipts. Notice her shoulders?'

'Yes, sir.'

'Of course. That's the thing about you, isn't it? You notice everything . . . Well . . .' He pursed his lips and raised his eyes towards the floor above where Forbes could still be heard whining. 'Not a prepossessing character, but we can't make a move at this stage. Not a mark on her, damn it. Still, there are the sleeping pills. No bottle, no prescription?'

'Not that I've found.'

'May have slipped her something. Well, a warning that

he's to remain at our disposal etc. then I must pay my respects to Eugenia.'

They forgave her, individually and jointly. Not, this time, for the wait while she searched for the keys to admit them, though that was considerable, but for having a little weep.

'I'll miss her.' She dried her eyes and tried to smile. 'In a lonely place like this and what with my leg . . . You count on your neighbours no matter what they're like, but I was so fond of Celia.'

'Someone to share your passion for books with.' Fusarri lit her cigarette for her. It turned out he was an old friend of the signora's late husband who had been a lawyer. It was all very cosy. The Marshal was choking on all the smoke and doing his best not to give way to a fit of noisy coughing and offend them. He was also so hungry he was in pain.

'What about him?' Fusarri asked, after finding a glass and pouring himself a drop of whisky which the Marshal once again refused.

'Oh, Julian. Well, he was very nice, of course . . .'

'He's not dead, Eugenia, only his wife is.'

'Even so, it won't be the same, you see . . . She didn't have a heart attack, that wasn't it?'

'No, we're pretty sure not. Why? Was her heart a problem?'

'Oh, I don't know. She never said so . . . I just remembered a friend of mine who had a heart attack in the bathroom and they didn't find her until the next day. Of course, she lived alone. Giorgio's always saying I should have someone living in and, of course he's right but I won't—Anyway, whatever he says I was right to call you, wasn't I, Marshal? But why . . . Oh dear, you must forgive me for being a curious old woman. I was going to ask you why her husband didn't call you and why he didn't answer the phone . . . I suppose I shouldn't ask these things but—'

'He was asleep, my dear Eugenia. Out cold on the bed, dead drunk. What do you think of that?'

Another tear escaped her blue eyes. She dried them and dabbed at her nose.

'Poor Celia.'

'Never an unkind word about anybody. You haven't changed. Nevertheless, you didn't like him and you might as well admit it, because the Marshal here misses nothing so you won't be able to hide anything from him!'

'Hide anything? Oh, Marshal, you don't think I was trying to hide anything, not seriously?'

'No, no . . .' Wretched man!

'I had nothing against him . . .'

'Eugenia, he's not dead.'

'No but . . . He often helped me, you know. He saw to the lemon trees this year because Giorgio hadn't time, and that was kind . . .'

'Eugenia!'

'Oh, you must forgive me, but you shouldn't speak ill— There I go again, I don't know what you must think of me, Marshal . . . Well, I'll be absolutely straight. He *often* did things for me. Sometimes he insisted on doing things for me that I wasn't altogether sure I wanted him to do. But Celia was a friend, I really felt that. She would help me if I wanted help, but mostly she just spent time with me— Oh, I don't know how to explain it exactly, but I just think Celia did things because she liked me whereas he . . . he did things so that I'd like him and that's the difference! You see, everybody liked Celia, she didn't have to do anything to make herself liked. She told me once he was jealous, not sexual jealousy. They'd actually had a row over some people they'd had to dinner because, according to him, their friends were not really their friends at all but *her* friends. He got drunk, I think, during the dinner and disappeared. She found him on the bed out cold. She said he'd drunk a lot before the meal—well, he must have done because he only got as far as the soup . . .'

Fusarri glanced at the Marshal.

'Must make a habit of it.'

'Oh, I don't think so,' said the Signora Torrini, 'Of course he could have done it on other occasions, but she only mentioned the one time.'

'Sorry, Eugenia, I was joking. It seems to be more or less what he did tonight, whether before or after his wife died we don't know.'

'I suppose if he was upset . . . I think I'll have another drop. Giorgio thinks . . . But I will. Just a drop—and oh heavens, who's going to tell Jenny? There's a daughter, Jenny, you know.'

'We didn't know. I don't think we knew.' Fusarri looked the question at the Marshal, who shook his head and wondered why the devil Forbes himself hadn't wondered who was going to tell his daughter.

'Hmph . . .' They both looked at him. 'Where is she? This daughter?'

'Jenny?' Signora Torrini rested her glass on her neat grey lap and thought for a moment. 'In England—I'm trying to remember where exactly—I'm afraid I forget names. But you'll see she'll be home tomorrow for half-term. Celia told me that.'

'Then her father will tell her,' Fusarri said. 'He'll no doubt have sobered up by then, eh, Guarnaccia?'

'He was always very good with Jenny . . . Oh dear . . .'

Fusarri decided to give up on reminding her which one was dead, only registering his observation by a wink in the Marshal's direction. But the Marshal didn't see it. He was frowning.

'Where does she sleep, this daughter, when she comes here? There's only one bed.'

'She stays next door at Sissi's now.'

'O my God, no! Don't tell me she's still going! Ah, Marshal, you have a treat in store—pity we can't go round there now. I'd like to have seen the old girl again. She must be ninety!'

'Ninety-one and going strong. She likes to have Jenny. It's company, you know, and they play piano duets together.'

Fusarri roared with laughter, which led to a fit of coughing.

'Really, Eugenia, this room is full of smoke!'

'Oh dear, you must forgive me. I do smoke a lot, but when I'm alone it doesn't matter . . .' She wafted ineffectually at the drifting clouds with a long pale hand, the nails well-manicured but unvarnished. 'I know what Giorgio would say and he's right—'

'Never mind Giorgio,' said Fusarri. 'You're going to suffocate the Marshal here who is the most precious element in this inquiry. Come along, Guarnaccia, I shall remove you from this den of iniquity and tomorrow you shall return and tackle the famous Sissi—what is the woman's real name, Eugenia?'

'Elisabeth obviously, but her surname . . . Wait a minute, I do know it—Müller I think . . . yes, it is. Müller. Are you really going? Oh dear, the keys . . .'

Fusarri, who had been careful to take them from her as soon as she'd finished locking everybody in, held them aloft with a wicked smile and blew a last smoke ring into the air. '*Les voilà!*'

It was very late when the Marshal climbed gingerly into bed in the hope of not waking his wife. But Teresa turned towards him half awake and then opened her eyes and sniffed.

'Where have you been? You reek of smoke, have you been in a night club or what?'

He didn't answer her and she turned away in a huff.

'Sorry I asked . . .' She was soon asleep again.

The Marshal's lungs were still full of smoke and he had to make an effort not to cough and wake her again. She would accuse him as usual of not telling her anything but in this case there was really precious little to tell. Also, he couldn't talk to her because if he opened his mouth, smoke or no smoke, she would detect the rest of that chocolate cake.

Vittorio's skinny legs didn't reach the floor, but you could see that however uncomfortable he was he daren't wriggle in the hard plastic chair. You could also see the scars on his knees quite clearly, but it was funny how the Marshal had forgotten that he never wore any socks. He must have been frozen in the winter, but nobody gave it a thought. It was just part of being Vittorio, not wearing socks. The judge was talking at great length, but no noise came out of his mouth and no one in the room seemed to expect Vittorio to listen or answer. The Marshal knew that at some point Sister Benedetta, though she wasn't there, would send the boy to kneel on rice in the corner of the classroom. But, though he had tried to look all around him, he couldn't see the corner where the rice should be. Of course this was a courtroom, so perhaps that was why.

'Marshal Salvatore Guarnaccia!'

The Marshal got to his feet and broke out in a cold sweat. They couldn't expect him . . . But though he opened his mouth to protest no sound came out and he too was on a red plastic chair. The worst thing was that the judge was now speaking to him, but however much he strained to catch the words they remained a distorted, blurred jumble. He reached towards the microphone, but withdrew his hand without touching it. That was surely for speaking into, not helping you to hear. From across the room Fusarri called cheerfully, 'Tell him about the husband being drunk! That's the best part!' The wonder of it was that neither he nor the Signora Torrini were smoking. But this was a courtroom, he reminded himself again, so they wouldn't be able to. That was his own voice he was hearing now. At least that was clear enough.

'On the spot evidence gave no indication that a crime had been committed. However, two capsules were found on the bedside cabinet of the deceased. These have yet to be identified. The body of the deceased, Celia Carter, born in Great Britain on February 12th, 1947, and resident in Florence at Villa Torrini, Via dei Cipressi, will remain at the disposal of the magistracy for further examination. On the orders of Substitute Prosecutor Virgilio Fusarri the body has been transported to the Medico-Legal Institute.

'Reserving the right to communicate further findings I enclose . . .'

The Marshal stopped dead. What was he talking about? You can't enclose things when you're being cross-examined. He'd muddled himself up with a written report.

'In any case,' put in the Signora Torrini, 'I'm all right now. They ran the water out of the bath and I went home. He's the one who's dead. Of course, I never did like him because of what he did to the lemon trees, but even so you shouldn't speak ill and when all's said and done he didn't do it. If you look at my neck and shoulders you'll see there isn't so much as the faintest bruise so he didn't push me under.'

The Marshal was about to point out that there was still the matter of the sleeping pills that could have been put in her drink until he realized with horror that Signora Torrini shouldn't have been there at all. Hadn't he just said the body was at the disposal of the magistracy? Fusarri was watching him, his eyes gleaming with suppressed mirth at the mess he was making. This was all Vittorio's fault!

'Why the devil did you have to dump this on me? Of all the places you could have taken that woman's body, why to Pitti?'

Vittorio's bruised eyes stared back at him without hope or interest. Though he didn't bother to open his mouth, the Marshal knew he was saying, 'I was frightened. I was always frightened.' His knees were bleeding, but he never mentioned that. Perhaps he didn't feel it any more. What he really wanted was a share of the Marshal's snack. It was his usual two giant slices of bread with mortadella, wrapped in brown baker's paper with spots of grease coming through. The trouble was he was so hungry himself and his mother had *told* him to eat it all. 'If you share it one day he'll expect it every day. I've enough trouble feeding you, never mind other people's children. He has a mother of his own, such as she is.'

But the Marshal couldn't bear the thought of Vittorio's mother. He held his big sandwich tighter and the grease came through on his fingers. He couldn't wipe them on his uniform. He was relieved, on looking down at himself, that it wasn't his uniform, but his black school tunic. Nevertheless, he couldn't face eating his sandwich with Vittorio's soulless eyes fixed on him. He'd have to hide somewhere, but where? He looked around the courtroom but there was nowhere they wouldn't be able to see him. Fusarri, the Signora Torrini, the judge . . . But worst of all Vittorio . . .

'You steer clear of that child. With a mother like that . . .'

Well, now he'd killed her. She'd been lying there drunk on Christmas Eve and he'd kicked her and kicked her with the others until they got frightened and dumped the groaning body on the Marshal, pretending to be passers-by. He'd thought at first, when he put the blanket over her as he waited for the ambulance, that he'd detected a pulse—

'You *thought* you detected?' inquired the Prosecutor with heavy irony. 'Was the woman dead or was she not?'

'I'm not a doctor,' protested the Marshal, 'I thought she might still be alive. She was badly injured but sometimes when people are drunk—'

'Pardon me for interrupting you, Marshal, but I seem to remember, the jury will no doubt also remember, that only moments ago you told us that it was the husband who was drunk! Not only drunk but drunk enough to be lying unconscious on the bed while his wife's body lay next door!'

Where had he gone wrong? He tried to consult the copy of his written report, but it was as blurred as the judge's voice had been because of the grease spots.

'I'm afraid—'

'You're afraid? I'm afraid, Marshal, that I shall have to ask for an adjournment, at least until after the autopsy!'

Everyone was leaving. Well, that was it, for now, anyway. The Marshal opened his eyes for a moment, registered the fact that he was in bed and dreaming, and then the fact that, dreaming or not, he was going to wake up to those same problems plus the diet.

'Blast!'

He sank back into unconsciousness.

CHAPTER 3

'It's mostly just a very sore throat and fever. I've kept him in bed . . .'

'It starts like that with everybody, but then it attacks the intestine, you'll see.'

'I never get the fever, I don't know how it is . . .'

The queue hardly seemed to diminish, not just because someone else always joined it as each customer left, but because everyone expected a bit of advice and commiseration along with an expensive package of ineffective 'flu remedies. Not many people called the doctor out, except for children, and a comfortable chat with the chemist or his wife was a perfectly good substitute—more cheerful, too, than the surgery.

The Marshal waited and watched. He wasn't in the 'flu queue, but sitting to one side where the chemist kept a café table and two chairs so that, during quiet periods, he could catch up on local gossip or talk politics. That was why the Marshal liked coming here. The shop was bright and in every other respect modern, but it was still a centre of information and a visit was always a social occasion.

'It's not what I gave you before, it's a bit stronger. See how you get on with it. Shall I give you something for your throat? . . . How's your mother's foot doing? . . .'

She was still a good-looking woman, the chemist's wife, and with her blonde hair she looked glamorous in her white coat. Mind you, her husband was a handsome man, slim and suntanned, never a grey hair out of place. The Marshal regarded him with envy as he approached—he must be at least eight or ten years older to look at him.

'There you are!' With a flourish, the chemist dropped a

box of capsules on to the table by the Marshal's elbow.

'That's the one.'

'Sleeping pill?'

'A common or garden sleeping pill. Overdose, is it?'

'I don't know.'

'In a screw of paper, you said? No box or bottle?'

'No . . . That's what's so odd.'

'You think so?'

'Don't you?'

'Not in the least. People are always passing out their medicines to friends, especially women. Is it a woman?'

'Yes. Yes . . . it was. She died.'

'And you think it might have been these?'

'I've really no idea. She was in the bath. Could have drowned. I'm just checking.'

'Well, you check her female friends and neighbours and you'll find I'm right. Aah . . . !' He sat down on the chair facing the door and stretched his legs. 'We could do with a sharp mountain wind to clean the 'flu away, but isn't it a treat when it's so quiet?'

The Marshal turned and glanced out at the little Piazza San Felice which was normally snarled up with traffic since it was a busy junction between four roads. The warm, over-cast weather which let the 'flu settle also let pollution settle, so that the alarms went off and the traffic would be banished from the city centre, like today.

'Trouble is, we like to ski at the weekends and there's no snow to speak of.'

So no wonder he was slim and tanned. The Marshal felt depressed and hungry. To cheer himself up he said, 'My two boys are off skiing with the school.'

'In Abetone?' It was where most Florentines went for convenience since it was in Tuscany.

'No, no . . . They've taken them further north, I forget the name of the place.'

'I gather it's the same everywhere. They manage to keep the pistes covered with the snow cannons and so forth but it's not the same. Keep these capsules if you need to.'

'If you wouldn't mind. I'll send them over to the Procura with these two . . . Would they be dangerous taken with alcohol?'

'Most drugs are dangerous taken with alcohol. Depends on the quantity, of course, though too rich a mixture of sleeping pills and alcohol usually provokes a fit of vomiting rather than a successful suicide. Mind you, someone sufficiently befuddled might well choke on the vomit.'

The Marshal remembered the bloody water draining away. If she'd vomited into it, the smell . . . A smell that reminded him of the drunken husband. He got to his feet.

'I'd better get out there . . .'

The chemist shook his hand. 'And remember what I said about the female friends.'

'I will. Thank you.'

As they drove away, young Fara said, 'I wish it was always like this.'

Thinking he meant the excitement of going out on a case, the Marshal said, 'Not much happens at Pitti. You'll have to be content with snatched bags and missing bicycles as a rule.'

'But . . . I meant the traffic.'

'Oh. Well, it's nice for us but it must be a nuisance for most people. Do you remember the way?'

'It should be easy enough in daylight. Excuse me, Marshal . . . Your seatbelt . . .'

'Eh? Hmph . . .' Female friends. He'd bet his life savings that it would turn out to be the Signora Torrini.

There hasn't been anything like that between them for some time. Celia tells me things.

And gets sympathy and a sleeping pill no doubt. If Forbes hadn't been sleeping with his wife he'd been going elsewhere. It was just what you'd expect from someone like Forbes, thought the Marshal, who was disgusted by him. Going elsewhere, that happened to most men lucky enough to attract women, but neglecting his wife was something else. If there wasn't enough to go round he should stop at home. A woman shouldn't have to turn to sleeping pills and tranquillizers and the like. It wasn't right.

'Marshal?'

'Eh?'

'I said, are you going to visit the signora you told me about last night? The one who apologizes?'

'No. Her next-door neighbour . . .' He got his notebook out.

'Signorina Müller.'

He had no intention of mentioning the sleeping pill business to the Signora Torrini unless the results of the autopsy made it inevitable—and then he'd leave it to Fusarri if he possibly could. Imagine if she really had something to feel guilty about and apologize for! There'd be no end to it. And as for what Giorgio would say . . . !

They wound their way up the broad avenue through trees that afforded an occasional glimpse of the red roofs and marble towers of Florence as they left it behind. Could stopping the flow of traffic have such an instant effect, or was the weather starting to change? At any rate a thin, watery sun was breaking through the greyness, producing just the sort of glare that hurt the Marshal's sensitive eyes most. Even behind his dark glasses they began to water slightly and he had to fish in his greatcoat pocket for a handkerchief to dry them.

Fara braked. 'Drat it . . .' Even though he'd seen the line of cypress trees he'd been looking out for, he'd still missed the turning, which came immediately after a bend in the road. He backed up and signalled left. 'It's a wonder we found it at all last night. What a place!'

Even in poor weather and in such an unlovely month, with its dead leaves and bare branches, the Villa Torrini was indeed quite a place. Not elegant or imposing like so many minor Tuscan villas which tried to compete with the Medici villas and failed. There was something very different about this house, something that suggested a home and not a showpiece. It had everything a country house ought to have, a paved yard, a loggia, a vineyard sloping gently down in front of it. But why was the peasant's cottage attached to the smooth stone villa instead of at a discreet distance? And the barn with its brick lattice-work only a metre away from that? Such a tiny barn, too, which in itself was unusual and smacked of country living for the joy of it rather than serious farming.

The Marshal got out of the car and breathed the damp grassy air. The weather, he thought, really was changing. There was a tiny breeze. An almond tree in the yard was just showing the tips of feathery pink blossom.

Fara got out, too. They found themselves, quite unconsciously, staring at the pretty miniature barn as though some ogre might suddenly burst from it. There was no sign of life there.

'Do you think he's in?' Fara's voice was almost a whisper in response to the quiet around them.

'How should I know?' growled the Marshal. But he did know, in the way that people always do know, though he didn't understand why it should be so. What is it about an empty house that tells you it's empty as you knock on the door or hold the telephone receiver, knowing no one will answer? You just know. In this case the Marshal knew that Forbes was in there somewhere and, what's more, he was watching them.

'He'll be sober by now, anyway,' Fara said.

'If he hasn't started drinking again.'

He had no intention of admitting it but the Marshal

had already decided that he wouldn't care to tackle Forbes sober, not without knowing just what the wife had died from. Nothing would budge him from the conviction that whatever that was, Forbes had something to do with it. But he'd be clever, much cleverer than any Marshal of Carabinieri. It was better to wait and watch.

'Aren't you going to talk to him at all?' ventured Fara, looking sideways at the Marshal.

'No.'

'I wonder what this old lady will be like. The one last night sounded quite a character.'

'This one, according to the Substitute Prosecutor, is worse.' But he didn't take Fara's obvious hint. 'Wait here and watch the barn.'

'Then you do think he's in?'

'Mph . . .'

'That's him!' It was only a movement. The lattice-work, which had been glassed in behind, didn't permit any clear view of what was inside. A pale flash that translated itself in their minds as a bearded face. 'He's watching us, I think.'

'Then you watch him.'

'He could feel he was being harassed.'

'I hope he will.'

The trouble with very old ladies is that they use their age as a weapon. They bully you with it and there's no defence. They remind you of it in a triumphant, accusing voice at every turn in the conversation. Not that you could call this a conversation. It was more of a lecture, interrupted at intervals by an examination, a test in comprehension and concentration which the Marshal failed miserably each time.

'You did say the Pitti Palace? I'm not deaf, you know, though I am ninety-one!'

'No, no . . . of course not. I did say the Pitti, yes. That's where I'm stationed . . .'

'Well then! You must have some opinion on the silver collection.'

'I—It's—I'm not a curator or anything like that . . .'

For God's sake! Perhaps she thought he was some sort of museum guard.

'I didn't think you were a curator since you presented yourself as a Marshal of Carabinieri. But you do have a pair of legs.' A glance at them suggested she didn't think much of them. 'The silver museum must be about two paces away from your office.'

'Yes, yes, it is . . .'

'Surely you've been there!'

'I . . . yes, but it's years ago,' he lied bravely.

'Prefer the paintings in the Palatine Gallery, I imagine,' she said drily.

'Not really . . .' He didn't want to have to answer questions on those.

'The arrangements there leave a lot to be desired. Barn of a place. You can't *see* the paintings. Been to Vienna?'

'No.'

You could see she thought he was a hopeless case but still she didn't give up on him. If only she would.

She was quite small and without any very definite shape under the knobbly greenish wool suit. She had hair that stood on end in a way that made her look at once alarmed and alarming, and the gimlet eye of a public prosecutor.

'Well, when you do go to Vienna, go to the Kunsthistorisches.'

'I will.'

'Good. You'll no doubt enjoy Bruegel's work. You're something of a Bruegellian figure yourself.'

The Marshal thanked her. She grinned at him wickedly, showing front teeth like a chipmunk's. The grin vanished as suddenly as it had appeared and the gimlet eyes narrowed. 'Well, we've established that you don't know much about Florence, young man, but we can hope at least that you know your job. Aren't you supposed to be investigating the death of Celia Carter?'

'Yes, that's why . . .'

'Well, if you don't mind my saying so, I think we should get on. At my age time is rather valuable.'

'Of course. I'm sorry. I came to see you because I understand their daughter stays with you when she's over here.'

'Yes!'

That was all. He was disconcerted.

'I . . .'

'Go on! I'm answering your questions.'

She had seemed such a chatterbox that he'd rather hoped she'd have volunteered some useful family gossip. Now it looked as though he'd have to question her like a suspect. He looked down at the gold flame on his hat, turning the hat round and round on his knee as he tried to formulate suitable questions so as to elicit suitable answers. It wasn't the way he liked doing things. The best information came spontaneously, but the Signorina Müller was only spontaneous about the history of art . . . He glanced at her. She, too, had lowered her eyes as though waiting submissively for his next question. Unable to believe in this submissiveness, he was bothered by the feeling that she might be making fun of him. But she looked very serious, solemn even. Her eyes remained lowered.

'Hm . . .' He coughed and made an effort. 'Did the daughter ever talk to you about the relationship between her parents? Were there problems with the marriage?'

She didn't answer. Possibly she was thinking it through. He prompted her gently.

'There could have been another woman . . .'

But Signorina Müller's chin dropped on to her chest. She

was fast asleep. She'd been fast asleep, he now realized, ever since the conversation had turned from history of art to other matters.

'Signorina . . . ?'

He waited, looking about him. The furniture wasn't what he was used to seeing. Perhaps she'd brought it with her from Vienna when she retired from being—of course—a museum curator. It was amazing to think that, if you worked it out, she'd been retired longer than he'd been working. She had every excuse, poor thing, for nodding off. He felt guilty for having tired her. She probably never saw anyone apart from her landlady, Signora Torrini, next door. And of course the girl Jenny when she was here. She wasn't here now. At least he'd managed to establish that before she'd taken over the conversation. Also, she wasn't any longer expected today. It was something. Apparently, she'd telephoned putting off her arrival.

Perhaps he should leave. She might sleep for an hour. It was very quiet. There was a huge ornate clock over the fireplace, but its hands were at twenty-five to six and probably had been for years. He glanced at his watch. He really had no objection to coming back another day. Ideally, he wanted some excuse to be here every day until he got the autopsy results so as to soften up that Forbes character, worry him as much as possible. There was nothing else he could do to him, though he must have realized when he sobered up that he no longer had his passport. It wasn't much, but it was something. That was a very nice piano. Open, too, and with music on it. More functional than the clock, obviously. Would you fetch a grand piano all the way down here from Austria? Though why not, after all? He'd brought all their furniture up from Sicily. Which was the greater distance? He wasn't at all sure.

'Is that all the questions you have?'

The gimlet eye was boring through him!

'Not that I object to your admiring my furniture.'

'I—'

'If you asked me a question I haven't answered, repeat it. I sometimes fall asleep but it doesn't last long. It's how I keep going. Don't imagine that I'm half-witted. That would be a mistake.'

'I wouldn't dream—'

'Get on, then.'

'I was asking you if you thought Mr Forbes had another woman. If he might have been in love with somebody else.'

This produced a snort of disgust. 'All this *love!*'

'You don't think so?'

'There are things I think about and things I don't think about. Incidentally, I don't care for Julian Forbes.'

'Neither do I,' admitted the Marshal. He shouldn't have, but he was fed up with being disapproved of. It was weak of him and it was unlike him. He put it down to hunger, which was gradually wearing down his personality.

'*She* was brilliant.' He took this to mean Celia Carter. 'A very rigorous historian—have you read her?'

The Marshal's heart sank. 'No, no . . .'

'You should. I'll lend you something.' She got up, pushing down on the arms of her chair but without taking too much time about it. Her books were in huge, glass-fronted cupboards.

'These are all hers on this shelf—Ah! This you should read: *Jessie White Mario and the Risorgimento.*'

She dumped the huge volume on his knees.

'You're sure you haven't read it? It has been translated into Italian, but I prefer books in the original language, myself. You don't disapprove of Jessie White Mario?'

'No,' said the Marshal emphatically. He was sure of that, at least, since he'd never heard of her.

'Well, some people do. One wonders about the husband, of course, but then, people will marry. Probably as much in love with Garibaldi as she was. Cavour, now, he's a man you have to admire but I can't like him, wily old goat. Freemason. That's what accounts for Garibaldi's circus making its way up the peninsula without impediment. No point in people throwing up their hands at what's going on in this country now. Whole state was founded on chicanery!'

'But you choose to live here?'

'Certainly. Finest artists and architects in the world. Never boring, either. That's important, don't you think?'

'I suppose . . .' If only she wouldn't hover and glare so much!

'Don't you have any more questions? I don't want to hurry you, but I'm going out shortly.'

'I'm sorry . . .' He stared down at the sepia photograph on the book's cover and decided on another line of attack. 'I think I should contact the daughter. I imagine you have her address and number?'

'Certainly.' She sat herself down at a writing-desk at the far side of the room and took out paper and pen. Then she turned back to him with a warning look. 'She'll be very upset.'

'Yes. Of course. It's natural, her mother . . .'

'Hmm.'

Probably her eyes weren't up to much. She bent her head so close to the paper, she was looking horizontally at the black pen as it crawled very slowly across the writing paper. As she wrote she muttered, 'She's bright enough and conscientious. She'd be considered very bright indeed if she hadn't such a brilliant mother to be compared with. Plays the piano rather pedantically. Too anxious . . .'

The Marshal waited, but this time he was quicker to notice that she was asleep, though no wiser as to what he should do about it. A cough didn't rouse her. Her head was nodding hardly an inch above the paper yet it didn't fall. He got up without a sound and approached the desk.

If she didn't wake he might try sliding the sheet of paper out from under her hand. She seemed to have written the address. As he bent over her he saw that, though her eyes were closed, she was smiling. At a movement of his hand towards hers the pen suddenly started scribbling again.

'Phone number . . .'

The Marshal retreated a step. 'Does she speak Italian?'

'I should hope so. It's what she's studying at university. There you are.'

'Thank you.' He was still holding the huge book along with his hat. 'Are you sure you want to lend me this? It looks valuable.'

'It is valuable, at least to me. Has the author's signature.'

'Exactly. The Signora Torrini was saying to me that she doesn't like lending books . . .'

'She lends them to me!' The chipmunk grin reappeared. 'Mind you, she keeps a list! A dear lady, La Torrini, but she hasn't much sense.'

'She doesn't like Julian Forbes,' pointed out the Marshal in her defence.

'I didn't say she had no taste.'

'What does he do, exactly?'

'Do? Hm! Affects to write books that never get finished, let alone published. First one was on Dante, or supposed to be. I lost track. Always managed to get himself socially accepted as a writer because of her. I don't care for that sort of thing, myself. Annoying. If you ask her a question about her books, *he* answers it. Did. That's over now, isn't it? La Torrini noticed the same thing but she never speaks ill of anyone. I speak as I find, but she's a good-natured soul.'

'She seems rather browbeaten by this Giorgio . . .'

'She brought him up.' She plumped back into her velvet armchair and eyed him sharply as he looked down at her. 'Not that I've any personal experience in these things, but

I imagine that, as in all areas of life, you reap what you sow. Families!' She evidently classed them with '*Love!*' 'I got out of my parents' house as soon as I could and I've never married. It's been a wonderful life. Ha!' The delighted grin vanished and she said, 'They're dangerous.'

The Marshal was rather taken aback by this remark.

'It's an intimacy that allows the most terrible abuse. The things that go on behind four walls! You'd be safer on a battleground. At least your enemy wears a different uniform. I suppose you're not old enough to have fought in the last war?'

'No.'

'I've lived through two. Unscathed. Precious little to eat, though—That reminds me, do you by any chance have television?'

'Yes. A television . . . yes.' Was that a good mark or a bad?

She seemed pleased. 'I don't, and of course you can't get a paper every day up here. I was wondering how things were in Russia.'

The Marshal dragged his memory without coming up with anything in particular. He stayed awake through the news, even Teresa would have to admit that. 'There's been no special news.'

'Things are as bad as ever, I suppose. I was there last month. Not much to eat and the problem with taxis . . .'

Her head fell gently forward, not all in one go but a little at a time. She must have begun dreaming before her eyes closed, confusing Moscow with wartime Austria. The Marshal settled his hat on his head and tiptoed out.

Fara had turned the car round ready to leave and was standing beside its open door staring at the barn like a pointer. Behind the Marshal a voice called softly, 'Have you a moment?' The Signora Torrini was in her doorway, leaning on her stick. He turned and went to her.

'You must forgive me. I'm wary of coming out in this damp weather because there can be wet leaves on the paving stones and I slip so easily. Giorgio's right, I should buy some robust shoes, non-slip, but we all tend to do and wear what we've always done and worn, don't you think?' She was wearing black court shoes.

'Yes, yes, you're right.' She was a welcome relief from her neighbour, despite all her apologies.

'I just wanted to tell you . . . it made me feel so guilty—you know how quiet it is here, just listen . . .'

It was very quiet. The few sounds, the distant bark of a dog, a nearby blackbird, the car radio crackling, only served to emphasize the quiet.

'Last night, I was reading—not reading properly, just dipping into one or two of Celia's books because I miss her company. It was like having her there, hearing her voice . . . Then I heard him . . .' She looked over at the barn and lowered her voice still more. 'He was crying. Not just crying, he was howling like a dog. I'm afraid I wasn't very kind about him yesterday but, you see, Virgilio provokes me and I can never deal with him . . .'

The Marshal, who felt the same way about Fusarri, nodded.

'He must be grief-stricken to howl like that, don't you think so?'

'Perhaps.' Privately, he thought Forbes might be howling in fear and self-pity, but in the face of Signora Torrini's more generous interpretation he couldn't bring himself to say so.

'He'll miss her terribly, you see, because she was an exceptional person.'

'Signorina Müller says she was brilliant.'

'Oh yes, well, she was, of course, but she was exceptional because of her good heart, her generosity. These things are so often taken for granted, even abused . . .' As though afraid of committing the sin of 'speaking ill' again, she stopped. 'You must have thought me very foolish last night to be talking about him in the past tense instead of poor Celia . . . but when I was reading I thought about that and, you know, there was some truth in it. She was everything for him, he'll be finished without her, I really feel that, whereas Celia lives on through her books. Do you understand?'

'I think so.'

'I'm afraid I'll still be lonely without her.'

'Well,' said the Marshal carefully, 'Signorina Müller seems quite a lively companion.'

'Oh, she is. But she's away so much, taking people round museums and so forth . . .'

'She takes people around Florence?' This boded ill. The Marshal imagined her storming his office and making him go round the silver museum.

'Oh no—well, sometimes she does, but not often. That would be nothing. At least, then, she's here in the evenings. No, she takes them all over the place. She spent all last month in Moscow showing people icons or something. Moscow in January, I ask you! But she says it's no colder than Vienna, which I suppose is true—Did she *lend* you that?' She had suddenly noticed the book.

'Yes,' admitted the Marshal unhappily, 'she did.'

'She must have taken a fancy to you. Oh, look at the almond blossom. Life goes on, doesn't it, Marshal? Whether you want it to or not.'

'And to cap it all, when we're driving away, Fara says "Don't look now but we're being followed. It must be your Austrian lady, it's not the one who came to the door."'

'And was it her?' Teresa got up to clear their plates.

'It was her all right. Stumping along in some sort of

Tyrolean cloak and a hat with a feather in it. She was shouting at us to get out of the way! It's true we were going at two miles an hour because of the potholes, but even so ... We had to stop in the end and let her pass. She glowered in at me and roared, "I always walk everywhere. Wouldn't do you any harm!" She was walking down to Florence. Can you believe it?'

'But ... This was this morning, wasn't it?'

He didn't answer. Lunch had consisted of greens, water and gloom. Only now, after a cleverly contrived supper, which had more or less filled him without endangering his liver, and a very small glass of wine which she had said would stimulate his digestion without doing him any harm, did he become almost expansive. He wasn't hungry but he didn't feel guilty. Also, the boys had telephoned, having stood in line for hours at the post office telephone in the village. They had complained bitterly. Just because they'd got excited and spent the night giggling and shouting and going up and down in the lifts and in and out of each other's rooms, the teacher had taken their ski-passes off them. So they'd spent the day toiling up the mountain for hours to ski down it for two minutes. They were exhausted and were going straight to bed. Giovanni had eaten three pork chops for supper. They were clearly having a wonderful time. The Marshal, who had never had a holiday in all of his young life, was pleased.

He had remained alert throughout the eight o'clock news in case anything happened in Russia. Now, after the half glass of wine which acted on his deprived organism like half a bottle, he felt he had life under control. While they waited for the water to boil for camomile tea at bedtime, he and Teresa looked at the fascinating old photos reproduced in Celia Carter's book.

'It's a shame it's in English but it was a kind thought to lend it to you.'

'She took a fancy to me.'

He went to bed happy and slept well. The next day his troubles began.

CHAPTER 4

'But . . .'

'Don't take it as final. I still need to examine the other internal organs but the stomach was empty, completely empty, so you can forget your sleeping pills. She hadn't even taken a sip of whatever was in the glass that broke in the water.'

The Marshal sensed that the pathologist was as surprised as he was.

'You don't think her heart . . .'

'No, I don't. I'll examine it, of course, but there are no symptoms. No, Marshal, all I can offer you is a very small quantity of soapy water which barely got into her lungs. Drowned in a glass of water as the saying goes, but it's a thing that normally only happens to babies and very small children. More choking than drowning, technically. I'd say it was impossible if I didn't have the evidence to prove it.

'Could he somehow have held her—'

'No, no, no. If someone pushes you under water you hold your breath and you fight for your life. It takes time to drown and you'd need enormous strength to do that to someone adult. Besides, there isn't a mark on her neck or shoulders, not the faintest sign of a scratch or bruise.'

'Nor on him.' That had been easy enough to ascertain since he'd been out cold when they found him. 'I only checked his hands and face . . .'

'Where else would you check? He was dressed, wasn't he? In any case his hands would be practically all she could reach. They'd have been in ribbons.'

'She did have nails? I mean, they weren't bitten down or anything?'

'No. Besides, we've removed whatever was under them as a matter of routine. You can't rule out someone else's possible presence entirely, I presume.'

That was true. Nobody had seen another person but there was no proof . . .

'Would you mind if I came out there?'

'Want to see for yourself, eh?'

'No, no, I wouldn't dream . . .'

'I was only joking. Help you to get your thoughts in order. I understand.'

Thoughts. The Marshal only wished he had any thoughts. He didn't understand anything about this business except that he didn't like Julian Forbes. And that didn't make the man a murderer, for goodness' sake. If the internal organs were found to be healthy there would be nothing for it but a verdict of accidental death.

'And that fellow lying there drunk!'

'What?' Fara, driving him out to the Medico-Legal Institute, had up to now seen the Marshal only as a kindly, if grumpy, father figure who'd made his first year in the army rather more comfortable than it would otherwise have been. Now he was disconcerted by this new version. He was silent for ages and didn't hear if you spoke or asked him something. Poor Fara, never having had occasion to go there, wasn't at all sure how to find the Medico-Legal Institute. His inquiries had been ignored and it was fortunate for him that once they reached hospital city at Careggi everything was signposted.

He peered about but could see no drunk.

'Do you want me to stop?'

No answer. Perhaps it was because he was on a diet. Fara knew all about the diet. Everybody at the Pitti Station knew all about the diet. And he'd heard it could do strange things to your brain, not eating.

'We're here, Marshal.'

'Eh? Ah.' He got out and stumped inside the large white building, removing his hat as he went. Fara shrugged and drove on to turn the car.

'There we are. Haven't quite finished sewing her up yet. You're not squeamish? We can wait if you'd prefer it.'

The Marshal shook his head and the pathologist sent his assistant away. The thorax was still open but the scalp had been sewn back in place. Until now, the Marshal had only seen her soaked from the bath water. Her hair had dried to a lightish brown and was wavy. It was spread in the dissecting trough now, but probably it had just touched her shoulders. There were grey hairs above her ears.

She was brilliant, Signorina Müller had said, but by now they had taken away her brain. She had been an intelligent, mature woman and she had drowned like a baby . . .

'Why is it,' he asked the pathologist who had parked himself on one corner of the table, arms folded, rubber gloves held in one hand, 'that babies drown like that?'

'Like I said, it's more choking than drowning, maybe in a few inches of water, maybe on their own vomit, sometimes in ways that remain undefined. You must have heard of so-called cot deaths. A baby's helpless, can't lift its head or move or signal for help.' He shrugged. 'What can I say? I can tell you what she died of—asphyxiation—but the how and the why . . . I'm afraid you'll have to sort that one out.'

'I'd like to know how with no evidence.' The Marshal's face was dark with displeasure. Then, remembering he wasn't addressing one of his carabinieri, he added, 'I beg your pardon. It's just such a funny business. Not clear cut.'

'Well—' the pathologist slid down from the table and got hold of Celia Carter's blue-white hand, turning it in his own and looking at her wedding ring—'the usual theory is the husband did it unless there's proof to the contrary.'

'If anybody did it at all. If it wasn't really an accident.'

The pathologist looked up at him. 'You don't believe that.' It was a statement, not a question.

'No. No . . .'

'I must say, I don't either. I wish I could offer you something that would help.'

But he couldn't. The Marshal had himself driven back to Pitti without saying a word. He'd been too complacent, sure that the autopsy would show up a murder which would have cleared his path for a thorough investigation of Forbes. Well, he'd been wrong, and having been wrong he'd wasted time. He should have been looking for the other woman, finding out what the man inherited, establishing a motive. He should have been doing all this in any case, so that, if the autopsy results had been useful, he'd have been ready . . .

They were stuck in a traffic jam near the banks of the Arno, contributing their share to the build-up of pollution that would lead to another alarm, another quiet day, another rapid build-up.

A beggar, walking among the waiting cars with his cap, saw the two uniformed men in the dark car and slid away. Windscreens were being washed at high speed. The Marshal stared out at the blue-grey world from behind his dark glasses and continued to castigate himself for being too slow, just as, all his life, he had been castigated by everyone, at home, at school, at work, for being too slow. Teresa, too . . . 'It's like talking to a wall! I asked you half an hour ago . . .'

The lights changed, but they didn't get through.

'Have they found out how she died?' Fara's timid voice floated on the edge of the Marshal's consciousness as he condemned himself out of hand for being a non-listener, asleep on his feet, too dozy altogether to tackle a type like Forbes even in his present reduced state—and Fusarri would have the preliminary notes on the autopsy, too. What

about that? He'd cottoned on right away to the fact that
the Marshal suspected Forbes, so now, either the Marshal
looked a fool or the Prosecutor looked a fool for believing
him. He hoped the former, because otherwise ... He'd
never seen the man angry, but he'd heard stories: that he
was an anarchist, that he overrode anyone who stood in
his way. Anyone. He'd even defied the chief public prosecutor once, if such stories were to be believed. They weren't
always, of course, but the Marshal, being only a non-
commissioned officer, didn't fancy his chances. And the
worst of it was that he was quite sure in this case that what
had sent everything haywire was his having been hungry
all the time. Diets were all right on holiday, but when you
had a job to do ... That Mercedes with a Calabrian
number plate had been parked there every day for a week;
he'd better take a closer look at it next time he passed on
foot. Incongruous ... And a house just further down where
there was some heavy gambling going on which meant
recycling money. He'd check ...

They were in Via Santo Spirito and another queue. The
best thing would be to go over to Headquarters at Borgo
Ognissanti and have a word with his captain. Captain Maestrangelo was a good man, a serious man, and he'd had to
deal with Fusarri. True, the Marshal had been there himself
at the time but very much in the background. Maestrangelo
had taken the brunt, and it hadn't been easy. Even so,
things had seemed to work out, more or less, in the end,
so a word of advice wouldn't come amiss. Borgo Ognissanti,
then—No, after lunch. A good meal would ...

If only he didn't keep forgetting! If only every day his
stomach didn't react joyfully to the peal of bells, the lunch-
time news signature tune, the waft of tomato and garlic
from the lads' kitchen upstairs, the clatter of cutlery behind
every shutter in every flat in every street. And then the
tightening with dismay. Might as well go straight over to

Borgo Ognissanti for all the difference a chilly salad would make. Borgo Ognissanti it was, then.

It was with some surprise that he found himself delivered to the gravel patch outside the entrance to his own station at the Palazzo Pitti. He kept his patience, though. His patience with the young and inexperienced was inexhaustible.

'No, no . . . Borgo Ognissanti. I want to see the company commander. Didn't you hear what I said? Don't look like that, it's not the end of the world. Just keep your eyes and ears open more . . .'

They crossed back over the river.

'Don't go in, I'll get out here. You go and eat and I'll walk back. Do me good.'

Fara's face was pink. He was perplexed and embarrassed. He drove back to Pitti thinking that before things got any worse he should try and find someone who could give him a word of advice.

Captain Maestrangelo was, indeed, a serious man. Journalists on the local paper, *La Nazione*, referred to him—though not to his face—as The Tomb. A nickname indicative both of his solemnity and the amount of chat and information to be extracted from him.

Nevertheless, it would be an even more serious man who could resist just a flicker of amusement at the sight of Guarnaccia, hands planted squarely on his big knees, a deep furrow between his brows, come to confess that he'd failed to solve a most intractable case in one and a half days. The flicker was an internal one. The Captain had no intention of offending the Marshal for whom he had a respect which Guarnaccia would not have believed had he known about it. Besides, he'd already guessed where the real problem lay, and that Guarnaccia would get to the point. Eventually. Over the years he'd become accustomed to the Sicilian baroque as expressed by the Marshal. The longest, most complicated line between points A and B. It was a slow business, but experience told him it got slower if you tried to block a curlicue and nudge him towards the horizontal. The result was invariably a flourish of minor curlicues to cover the embarrassing glimpse of the horizontal pointing straight at point B. Sometimes, the Marshal lost his way in the minor curlicues. So the Captain held his peace apart from suitable murmurs on request.

'After all, if he does have another woman, he must have friends who know . . .'

'Surely.'

The Marshal gazed down at his hands for some time and then emitted a brief sigh that was almost a snort.

'And money . . . I don't know what a writer would earn . . .'

'No.'

'But there could be money, family money. The daughter hasn't turned up yet and, of course, I can't even be sure there wasn't someone else there. Though you'd think if there had been, Forbes wouldn't have lost an opportunity to shift the blame. He was drunk, though. It's a funny business . . . man lying drunk next door to his wife's body.'

He consulted his hands again. The Captain, very discreetly, consulted his watch. But still he held his peace.

'Not a mark on her. Not a scratch or the tiniest bruise. And nothing at all in her stomach, clean as a whistle. So why should a perfectly healthy young woman faint or something . . .'

'Perhaps because of the empty stomach. Women go on excessive diets sometimes, I believe.'

The remark had the effect of an electric shock on the Marshal. He sat bolt upright, his face red. 'I never thought . . .'

'Well, I wouldn't get too hopeful about it, just check it out.'

The Marshal sat there looking stunned.

'I know it must be difficult for you,' prompted the Captain against his better judgement. 'It's a bit much for you to take on when your only really experienced man is Lorenzini and he has to be in the office when you're out. I'd send you someone if I could—I know what it's like when you're feeling under pressure from a prosecutor who forgets you've also got a whole Quarter to police—'

'No, no,' protested the embarrassed Marshal to his shoe. He then fixed his gaze on a seventeenth-century landscape in oils on the wall to his left and discoursed doggedly on staffing problems for seven minutes.

The Captain felt he was losing his grip. He'd done precisely what he knew he shouldn't have done and, after all, it was perfectly comprehensible that the Marshal couldn't bring himself to come here openly protesting about the Substitute Prosecutor he'd been given, like a schoolboy unhappy with his new teacher.

With tact and patience the Captain picked up the responses and they wound their way in the correct form with all due curls and ornaments, through past staffing arrangements, acquaintances now transferred, cases this or that one worked on, until they came upon, after a decent interval, a certain kidnapping case and a certain substitute Prosecutor Virgilio Fusarri, then newly arrived in Florence.

'And does he still smoke those dreadful little cigars?' asked the Captain after feigning surprise that he was on this case.

'Chain-smokes. And . . . the owner of the Villa Torrini where it happened, smokes as much as he does. Cigarettes, though. They're old friends . . .'

'Is that going to be a problem?'

'I don't know. I don't think so, but you never can tell.'

'Well, if it isn't, I wouldn't worry about him too much.
I know his manner's very strange . . . That way he has of
being only half with you, taking an amused interest, like a
privileged spectator whose real business is elsewhere. The
only time I've seen him really concentrate is on food.'

'Yes, well.' That didn't strike the Marshal as altogether
unreasonable. 'It's more the way he pretends to flatter me
that's disturbing. All this "leaving it to me".'

'Perhaps he means it.'

'Hmph. And if it all goes badly?'

'I really don't think you should worry. I confess I felt
the same way about him in that respect, but I have to
admit that when things got difficult he stood by me.'

The Marshal stood up. He still looked unhappy.

'I shouldn't be taking up so much of your time.'

'I'll walk down with you. I have to go out anyway.' He
rang for his adjutant and ordered a car.

They walked the polished monastic corridor in silence.
Below them in the cloister a squad car was revving up. In
the old refectory, which ran the length of the opposite wing,
off-duty lads were playing table tennis.

On the stone staircase the Captain said, 'If it makes you
feel any better, I remember him telling me that you were
a good man, reliable.'

It didn't make the Marshal feel any better.

'The only thing that needs watching,' added the Captain,
'is the business of his being so friendly with the Torrini
woman. No point in treading on anyone's toes if you can
avoid it. There's a reception tomorrow night—the Mayor,
the Prefect and so on. My colonel's going. He's the right
sort and I'm sure he'll check which way the wind's blowing
for me—where's your car?'

'I sent it back. Need a breath of fresh air.'

Walking back up Borgo Ognissanti, the Marshal realized
that he did feel better—not about Fusarri, he couldn't do

with Fusarri at any price—but about getting this investigation sorted out in normal terms. He was grateful for the advice the Captain had given him. He'd be even more grateful if the Captain had taken the whole business off his hands. You needed an officer, an educated man, to deal with someone like Forbes. Mind you, that was hardly an excuse for him, of all people, not to have thought of the woman being on a diet. Blast this tepid, sickly weather!

He had reached the Piazza Goldoni which opened on to the river bank and his eyes were streaming. He'd forgotten to put his dark glasses on. Damn! He paused under the statue to fish for them in his greatcoat pockets. He'd never gone and left them . . . No. They were there. The plump playwright looked politely the other way with a little smile on his face as the Marshal gave the glasses a polish with a clean white handkerchief and dabbed his eyes dry before putting them on.

He set out across the bridge. The Arno was brown and swollen from the recent rains. It wasn't that much of a pleasure, walking with so much traffic streaming past, and as for breathing fresh air—it was ninety per cent exhaust fumes. And the noise . . . someone was shouting above it.

'Glad to see you taking my advice! Hallo! Hallo!'

A Tyrolean hat had popped up at the level of his breast pocket, forcing him to back up against the parapet. At once he was surrounded by bobbing, smiling faces.

Signorina Müller's chipmunk teeth were in full festive view: 'Out for a stroll! Good! We haven't much time, ourselves. Got a minibus waiting over at the Excelsior car park to take us up to the Certosa. I suppose you've seen the Pontormo frescoes a hundred times or I'd invite you. This is Marshal Guarnaccia. Can't get him interested in silver, but he's very fond of paintings. He's at the Palazzo Pitti. Now: this is Professore Tomimoto of Kyoto University.'

In stunned silence the Marshal held out his hand.

Professore Tomimoto, ignoring it, bowed.

'And Professoressa Kametsu.'

The Marshal's hand wavered and withdrew.

Professoressa Kametsu bowed.

'And their students.' The students bowed and smiled.

'Delighted to see you getting some air, Marshal. How did you like the book?'

'Ah . . .'

'A brilliant writer. We shall miss her. Spoken to the girl?'

He had to think a moment before he got there. 'The daughter? No, not yet.'

'She should be here. Have to come to the funeral. You come back and see me. There are things I'd like to talk to you about. Must get on.'

She got on, stumping along on her heavily-shod feet. The professors and their students all bowed courteously and got on, too.

The Marshal, watching them go, thought that sometimes she must fall asleep during these outings, perhaps in front of a painting, perhaps even at the traffic lights, but that those polite people would never mention it.

He hadn't, he recalled, asked for any advice about Signorina Müller from the Captain who was always more dismayed by bullying old ladies than he was. Besides, he fancied he was beginning to like her. Before leaving the bridge, he gave a hopeful glance upriver in search of the purplish blue stripe that formed across the horizon when the mountain wind was on its way. Nothing. The ochres and reds of the Ponte Vecchio were muted, the hills beyond screened by mist. Well, as long as it arrived before he caught the 'flu. He'd been lucky up to now, he'd escaped with only a heavy cold at the end of November. Unconsciously, he quickened his pace as though to prevent the virus from catching up with him.

*

'Just don't imagine he's angry with you, even when that's the way it looks.'

The Marshal had left his young brigadier, Lorenzini, in charge of his office, and at five o'clock he was in there talking. The Marshal hesitated at the door, not sure whether he was on the phone or had somebody with him, not wanting to interrupt if he could help it. There was definitely somebody in there, but so quietly spoken he could only hear a faint murmur of distress without distinguishing the words.

Lorenzini sounded sympathetic. 'I know, I know, but it's nothing personal. He gets like that and there's no point in telling him because he doesn't hear, let alone answer.'

More murmurs of distress. The Marshal took his glasses out and gave them a rub before slipping them back into his pocket. A coffee wouldn't come amiss when Lorenzini had got rid of whoever was in there.

'I'm sure you have—and the other thing is, that when it passes off there's still no point in talking to him about it because he can't remember and wouldn't believe you. You just go about your business—and keep your eyes open because, however much he seems to be bumbling about . . . I was going to say he knows what he's doing, but of course he doesn't. Only he'll do it. And you might learn something even without the aid of the spoken word. And cheer up! It's better than being stuck inside all day, isn't it?'

A great talker, Lorenzini. Good at dealing with people, especially foreigners . . . knew a fair bit of English, too . . .

The Marshal showed his face at the duty room door.

'Everything all right?'

'Fine.' Di Nuccio was alone at the radio switchboard.

'Where's young Fara?'

'In with Lorenzini, won't be long.'

'Oh . . . ? Ah, here he is.'

Fara's face turned beet red when he saw the Marshal, who stepped back to let him into the duty room and at once turned away to talk to Lorenzini.

'Can you prepare a package for me for the Prosecutor's office while I get the paperwork done?'

'What size?'

'It's only a couple of capsules—oh, and put in this complete pack of them the chemist gave me. Save them a bit of time at the lab if they check against those—By the way, what's the matter with Fara? Not getting himself in any trouble, is he?'

'No, he just wanted a bit of advice . . .' Lorenzini's eyes searched the Marshal's face and, finding it blank, felt free to add, 'Just feeling a bit homesick, really.'

'Well, he'll soon get over that—though I must say these boys these days don't look old enough to be here. That must be me getting old, mustn't it?'

'I'm afraid so.' Lorenzini smiled. 'It's happening to me, too, now, ever since we had our little boy. Must be paternal feeling at the root of it. The photos and house plan for the Torrini case have come, by the way, so if you can get through the reports we can have it all ready to go off by the time we shut shop.'

'*If* I can get through them . . .'

He just about made it. He did the search report and the receipts for the passport and capsules first, and then opened the packet of photographs in the hope of seeing something he hadn't seen, noticing some detail he'd overlooked. There was nothing. The perfumed suds on the cold pink water, the sightless eye turned towards him just above the surface. His own hand was still in the first picture after they'd turned her. The broken glass embedded in her buttock: it hadn't killed her. Whatever it had contained, she hadn't drunk from it. Why was it underneath her, though? He tried to imagine dropping a glass into the bath and the glass breaking. Well, you'd get out, wouldn't you? You wouldn't sit there fishing for the pieces, you'd get up . . . and slip perhaps and cut yourself—and wouldn't you scream? Or faint . . . whichever you did you'd make some commotion and Forbes—Forbes wasn't drunk, not yet he wasn't. They'd just come in and Signora Torrini saw them. She'd have said—or would that come under the heading of speaking ill of the as good as dead? He'd have to ask her. One thing he could check in the meantime. He called the Medico-Legal Institute.

'No, I'm sorry, he's not. Can I be of any help? I'm his assistant . . . yes . . . yes, I did—no, there's no need, I remember quite well that the cuts were post-mortem—there was a fair bit of seepage, the cuts being on the underside and immersed in water, but nothing like the bleeding such deep wounds would have caused had she been alive. Anything else? Not at all.'

A dead end. The diet, then. The only person he could think of to ask about that was the Signora Torrini, but she didn't answer her phone though he let it ring and ring, knowing that it might take her a long time to get to it. Odd. He'd been under the impression that she didn't go out, though of course the famous Giorgio must occasionally show up and perhaps take her somewhere. Well, if that was the way it was he would ask Forbes himself at some point. The idea didn't please him. He was still of the opinion that he would rather anyone but himself asked Forbes anything. He allowed the Signorina Müller to cross his mind briefly and dismissed her from it. It would almost certainly be one of the things she did *not* think about. He could imagine her reaction: 'Diets!' and the instant removal of the conversation on to a higher plane.

There was nothing for it. He began to type.

On arrival at the scene the presence of a cadaver in the bathroom of the habitation described in the enclosed plans was established . . .

The thing was to cover yourself for all eventualities. Tongue between his teeth, two plump fingers picking out the letters, he wrote:

From the on the spot evidence obtained, at the present time, no hypotheses of any specific crime emerge.
Reserving the right to communicate the results of my further inquiries I enclose:
—Death certificate.
—Search report.
—Sequestration report for two medicinal capsules.
—Sequestration report for the passport of FORBES JULIAN.
—Photographic file.
—Statements obtained from TORRINI EUGENIA *and* MÜLLER ELISABETH.

'Marshal?' Lorenzini tapped and came in with the package as the Marshal put his signature to this report which listed everything and concluded nothing.

He accepted the small box tied up with string. 'Ask one of the lads for a lighter, would you?'

Lorenzini held up a black plastic lighter between two fingers. 'Done'.

'Ah. You go home, it's late. This can all be sent to the Prosecutor's office tomorrow. He'll hardly be there at this time.'

But the Marshal was wrong. As he let the hot red wax drop on to the string of the parcel, his phone rang.

'Damn!' Whoever it was had to wait until he had melted enough wax and had a hand free. It was Fusarri.

'Glad I caught you. I gather you've been at the Medico-Legal Institute. Bad news, eh?'

The Marshal, thinking it somewhat improper to give voice to the idea, said nothing. This only made Fusarri laugh. 'Now then, Marshal, don't tell me that a stomach containing a suitable mixture of alcohol and sleeping pills wouldn't have been as welcome to you as it would have been to me.'

No point in angering the man unnecessarily.

'Yes, sir. He would have said it was suicide, of course.'

'Of course. But better than nothing, which is what we've got now. You think he did it.'

'At present,' quoted the Marshal, referring unhappily to the report on his desk, 'no hypotheses of any specific crime—'

'Oof! We shall have to find one. Go and see him. Take his statement.'

'I thought perhaps that you—'

'No, no, no. You're the man for it.'

The Marshal's heart sank. Remembering just in time, he reached for the seal and pressed the State symbol and *Carabinieri Tuscan Region Palazzo Pitti Station* into the cooling red wax.

'Are you still there?'

'Yes, sir. I'll go tomorrow morning.'

'Excellent. I gather he's an intellectual type. He'd try to talk all over me. Pah! I don't think he'll be able to do that to you. Pity I can't be a fly on the wall for this meeting of two diametrically opposed minds, but there it is. Tell him I'm issuing a release order for the body. He can bury his wife.'

'And his passport . . . Should he ask, I mean.'

'Oh no! He's not getting that. Make the proper excuses, bureaucratic delays, everything under control, matter of days, all that stuff. By the way, there's money, I believe, quite a lot of it. I've had a solicitor round here—but don't you worry about that, I'll deal with it and inform you.'

'Thank you.'

Could it be that the Captain was right? That perhaps

Fusarri—but no. 'Meeting of two minds!' He could only be making a joke of him.

'Not at all. It'll involve a few calls to England. Your talents are better employed elsewhere. You talk to Forbes. I rather think you'll frighten him.'

'I . . . *frighten*?'

'Do you wear those dark glasses of yours all the time?'

'It's an allergy I have,' the Marshal defended himself, 'the sunlight hurts my eyes.' What the devil . . . ?

'Good, good.' He rang off.

It wasn't right. Somebody eccentric like that—it wasn't right. You needed serious men in this sort of business, men like Captain Maestrangelo. It just wasn't *right*.

CHAPTER 5

A log fire was burning in the wide hearth. The Marshal was glad of it since there was no other heating in the converted barn. It hadn't been lit long, and every so often a fine curl of pale blue woodsmoke made its way up one corner of the mantelpiece. The sweetness of its perfume mingled with that of the freshly made coffee which the Marshal had reluctantly refused. He didn't want to accept anything from Forbes. He wasn't sure whether Forbes had just got up, or was making the coffee to give himself something to do other than sitting down and facing his visitor. Probably a mixture of the two.

There was a long-haired white rug in front of the fire which the Marshal kept his big black shoes away from. A very cosy room, though he wondered about the strength of the piece of bamboo furniture on which he was gingerly sitting. Pretty but frail, he thought, trying not to move an inch. When he did, it creaked.

Forbes was talking. He'd hardly drawn breath since the Marshal arrived. Talking mostly about himself. The Marshal wasn't listening—at least not to the content, only to the noise, the accent, the tone, the fear. When Forbes did at last present himself at the fireside, he brought with him two cups of coffee.

'You were only being polite, right?'

And after that it would have been an exaggeration not to drink it. Blast the man! Hadn't the Signora Torrini said that Forbes did things for her even though she didn't really want him to, so as to make himself liked? He understood that now. He had very much wanted the excellent coffee, but he hadn't wanted it from Forbes. Probably, the Signora

Torrini had wanted her lemon trees protected but she wanted it done by her son. No doubt Forbes had done a good job. He had also made good coffee. Which made matters worse. How he talked! He was in the bamboo armchair opposite now, legs crossed one over the other, a long delicate finger caressing his beard and his elbow poised on one knee. The knee was shaking. Only very slightly, but it was shaking.

He was losing his hair very quickly, the Marshal thought, looking at the receding temples and remembering the almost bald crown. Yet he looked young. Perhaps because his skin was so soft and pink, as was often the way with northern people.

'In this job you can't allow your emotions to interfere or you're out. I have a deadline to meet.'

'Job . . . ?' The Marshal came briefly to the surface. As far as he knew, Forbes had no job.

'This article I'm writing for an English Sunday. The deadline's tomorrow. I'm trying to work in spite of everything. She would have wanted it.'

The Marshal stared at him. He took a sip of the coffee without thinking and then, annoyed with himself, placed it on the low bamboo table between them.

Again he looked hard at Forbes before announcing: 'I'm here to tell you—' Forbes had never asked why he was here—'that Substitute Prosecutor Fusarri has signed a release order for your wife's body. You might wish to bury her tomorrow or the next day at the latest.'

'I can't. My friends, a couple we know—she's English and he's Italian—they're going to see to everything for me. They think a lot of me and they know I need to write this piece and I can't deal with things like that.'

'There comes a time in all our lives,' pointed out the Marshal, 'when we have to deal with "things like that". Are they friends of yours, these people, did you say, or were they friends of your wife's?' Signora Torrini might be daffy but she'd got this chap sized up, and very useful it was, too.

Forbes's face was red with annoyance. 'Mine, if anything. Especially Mary, the wife. To be honest . . . well, she's always been a bit in love with me. These things happen, you understand, in certain circles. They're accepted.'

Very nice, the Marshal thought, particularly if it results in someone else organizing your wife's funeral for you.

Forbes sat back elegantly in his bamboo armchair and opened one hand in an adopted Italian gesture.

'I shouldn't have brought it up. I realize it's difficult for someone like you to understand. There are different standards in different ambiences.' The flourish of the hand was perfectly controlled but the Marshal knew without needing to look that the leg swung over his knee was still shaking and that the foot was tapping at the air to cover it up.

'Very nice furniture, this,' he said to try and cover up a sinister creak, the result of his shifting a little, to observe Forbes better.

Forbes was disconcerted, and the further speeches he was working up to on the question of different ambiences disintegrated on the spot. The Marshal was equally disconcerted at having started a hare when least expecting to. The furniture seemed to agitate Forbes a great deal more than the funeral.

'It was meant to be a surprise, that was the whole idea— it was a *present* and yet you'd think—who told you about it anyway?'

'Told me about it?'

'Somebody must have—La Torrini, I imagine, I know you went to see her.'

'Yes, I did.' What was the matter with the man? 'We didn't discuss your furniture.'

'Fucking hell!' He suddenly turned his face and covered it with one hand. He was weeping.

The Marshal waited in silence. It wasn't just when he was drunk, then. Why, though, should he have burst into tears at the mention of his furniture? After some moments, a possible explanation occurred.

'You say these things were a present. Were they for your wife's birthday?'

Forbes pulled a handkerchief from his trouser pocket and blew his nose loudly. 'Sorry. No, not her birthday. For Christmas.'

'I see.' The Marshal watched him rub a hand over his face.

'I just thought you'd have bought something for your wife that day.'

'What day?' He was reaching for his coffee cup, pouring more from the octagonal pot he'd left close to the fire.

'The day she died. It was her birthday.'

He hesitated, almost dropped the coffee pot, burned himself saving it. 'Christ! I've burned myself!' He jumped up and went to the other end of the room which served as the kitchen. Still swearing, he opened the ice compartment of the fridge and put his hand inside.

'You'd forgotten?'

Forbes pretended not to hear.

'Have to put something on it . . .' He ran up the spiral staircase at a speed the Marshal wouldn't have thought possible. He was used to it, of course. He was running away from the question, too. Well, there was no hurry.

Even so, he wasn't finding out anything and perhaps he never would. He had no idea how to tackle this Forbes chap, and he was afraid his dislike was making itself felt. That could result in a complaint, protests from the consul, the ambassador . . .

He could hear Forbes fiddling about upstairs. He was

gone for quite some time and came back with his right
hand inexpertly bandaged by his left. The Marshal made
no comment on this, but continued, as though Forbes had
never moved.

'I was saying that you forgot your wife's birthday. I hope
she didn't take it too badly.'

'She didn't . . . know. I mean, she never mentioned it so I
suppose she'd forgotten it herself . . .' His eyes were shifting
rapidly about the room. The Marshal, trying to make out
where he was looking, concluded that he wasn't so much
looking at something as for something.

'Funny,' he said slowly, 'all her friends forgetting, too,
though if you forgot and they didn't, perhaps she avoided
saying. Women are like that, don't you find?'

'I've no idea,' snapped Forbes. 'If there's nothing else—
I did tell you I've work to do.'

'One or two things,' the Marshal said carefully to the
settling fire. He didn't move. He felt, rather than saw, that
Forbes's frantically seeking eyes had frozen. Settling back
just a little in his chair, he spotted it too. A brown leather
handbag. It was hanging from the back of a straight chair.

'I should explain,' he said, 'as you weren't feeling too well
at the time, and probably didn't notice, that our technicians
examined everything in the house for evidence—in particular, evidence of suicide. Note, pills and so on.'

Forbes fell silent. He thought for some time and then his
eyes glanced off the Marshal's as he tried to look him in
the eye, man to man, and failed.

'She always picked up the post. They leave it in a box
near the gate. That day she stuffed it in her bag. She said
there was nothing interesting . . .'

'Very tactful.' The Marshal took out his notebook.

'What are you doing?' said Forbes in alarm.

'Don't worry,' said the Marshal calmly, 'I'm not making
a note of the fact that you forgot your wife's birthday. But

last time I was here, you were in no state to give me a statement of the events of the day which ended in her death. Can I take it now? Did you quarrel that day?'

'No!'

'What time did you get up in the morning?'

'Early. At least I did. I started work on my article. Celia slept late because she'd had trouble getting to sleep.'

'Did that happen often?'

'I don't know . . . I only noticed if she told me and stayed in bed late. Otherwise I fall asleep as soon as my head touches the pillow.'

'You must have a clear conscience.' This was an attempt to be more pleasant, but he realized afterwards that he probably should have smiled or something.

'I work very hard!' One leg was still crossed over the other but he had ceased to affect relaxation with his arms, which were now folded tightly on his chest.

'And you worked very hard that morning. For how long?'

'I couldn't say. A couple of hours. Then we had something to eat.'

'What?'

'What did we eat? An English breakfast. I made it.'

'An English breakfast? What is that? Eggs . . . ?'

'Eggs and bacon, tomatoes, sausages, fried bread. We liked to do that sometimes and then work straight through to supper-time.'

'And your wife ate all that stuff?' Well, you never knew, it might be one of those favours he insisted on doing when all she wanted was a cup of coffee. 'She wasn't on a diet?'

'Why should she be on a diet?'

'Her stomach was empty when she died. What time did you have this English breakfast?'

'Tennish.'

That, he supposed, accounted for it, though he'd have to check with the pathologist. From ten to six she hadn't eaten. He made a note in his black notebook, taking his time over it, hoping for some reaction from Forbes but none came. He could hear talk of the pathology of his wife's death without a flicker and burst into tears over the furniture!

'And the rest of the day?'

'We were out. We went down into town to the post office. Then we split up. She went to get her hair done—they stay open over lunch and it's the quietest time . . .'

He bent to place two more logs on the fire and fidgeted with them for an unnecessarily long time. The Marshal waited in silence.

Forbes sat back abruptly. 'We met up when the shops opened and did—'

'Where were you?'

'What?'

'Where were you while your wife was at the hair-dresser's?'

'I went to see this friend—Mary. She's the one—'

'I remember.'

'She had some books I needed for my article. I wanted her to help me, that's all. She'd written something similar for the *Herald Tribune* so I thought I could save myself some research. Nothing happened.'

'Did you try?'

'No, I had other things on my mind.'

'And then?'

'Nothing. We did some food shopping and came home. Celia wanted a bath . . . a bath before . . .'

Beads of sweat began forming at his temples. He jumped up and poked the fire again, then sat down on the edge of his chair and refolded his arms tightly.

'Go on.'

'Nothing! I unpacked the shopping while she had a bath, that's all. That's all. When she didn't come out I shouted something. I wanted a bath myself, that was it—

I'd forgotten that—and she didn't answer, so I went in and she was there . . .'

'She didn't lock the door?'

'Of course not. Why should she, with just the two of us here? There isn't a lock . . .' The knee was tapping the air with amazing rapidity that could only be involuntary.

'Go on.'

'Go on what! I can't . . . I saw she was dead. She was dead . . .'

'And what do you think she died of?'

'I don't know, how could I? I mean, I thought a heart attack, something like that. What was I supposed to think? How do you think I felt?'

'I don't know. Most people would have called a doctor or at least a neighbour, asked for help.'

'I was too upset. I was in shock. I can't even *remember* now, that's how upset I was, can't you understand that?'

'So you had a drink. You were quite sure she was dead, were you? You checked her heart or pulse?'

Forbes looked horrified. About to speak, he suddenly stopped himself. His whole forehead was beaded now.

'She could have been alive. If you thought it was a heart attack you could have called the coronary unit out.'

'She was dead! What was the use if she was dead?'

'But you didn't check.'

'I couldn't touch her . . . I couldn't! I've never even seen anyone dead before, let alone touch—'

'And yet you're quite sure she was dead.'

'You know these things.'

'And so you drank a whole flask of wine.'

'I don't remember. I was upset. I started drinking.'

'What was in her glass?'

'Wine. It was wine. Sometimes she liked a gin and tonic at that time, but it was wine—and I poured it for her in the kitchen down here. She took it up with her.'

'And you didn't see her again until she was dead, or you thought she was.'

'She was dead.' He dropped his head into his hands and a stifled whine escaped him. 'Oh, why did this have to happen to me? Oh God, why?'

It happened, the Marshal thought, to your wife. He didn't speak the thought but backed carefully a little further away from the fire which was now roasting his knees.

'I understand your wife has left you provided for. And your daughter, of course.'

'She's not my daughter. She's Celia's daughter by her first husband.'

'I beg your pardon. I imagined . . .'

'Well, don't. Celia will have left her the London house, I know that.'

'She'll be here for the funeral?'

'Yes, and that's all.'

'I take it you didn't get on.'

'I didn't say that.'

'No, but if you don't want her here . . .'

'She's at university in England. She has a life of her own.'

It was only to be expected, the Marshal told himself. A man who doesn't feel sufficiently responsible to organize his own wife's funeral is hardly likely to want the responsibility of a daughter. Forbes had stood up. He was very agitated and tried to cover it by removing their coffee cups and himself to the other end of the room. The Marshal rather thought it must be costing him enormous effort not to run out of the house. The most he dared to do was to keep his back to the Marshal by washing and re-washing the two cups.

'I take it this is it? I mean, you've taken my statement and we can bury her. End of story, right?'

'Very probably. The pathologist has still to examine the internal organs before he can make his report.'

That produced no effect.

'I have to get on with my life. What's happened has happened, and I have to get on with my life.'

My life, thought the Marshal. My life, my article . . . It distressed him to the extent that he said Forbes's lines for him:

'How very sad,' he said to the burning logs, 'that your wife was unable to get on with her life, that a young woman of such brilliance should die like that.'

'Are you trying to imply that in some way I could have prevented it?' He still kept his back turned, fidgeting in the wall cupboard now.

'No, no . . .'

'Well, if that's all . . . There's nothing else I can tell you.'

The Marshal sat still, worried, uncertain, but immovable.

'Take your time,' he said, 'and when you've finished your chores you'd better tell me about the other Marys. I imagine there are others.'

One of the logs rolled off the burning stack and sent a spume of aromatic smoke curling out into the room. Forbes was still fidgeting out of sight. After a moment he reappeared by the fire.

'What's that got to do with anything?'

'Oh, just the usual routine, as much to rule out suicide as anything. An upset wife . . . we can't be a hundred per cent sure, as I said, until the pathologist makes his official report.'

'My private life has nothing to do with you or your pathologist. I have had other women, yes. Who hasn't? But never anything serious and I never intended to leave Celia, never.'

'And did she know about the other women?'

'Yes, she did. I told her.'

He would, thought the Marshal. He was just the sort to go confessing everything so that he'd feel better.

'And why did you do that?'

'Because I prefer relationships to be open. I wouldn't have felt happy about hiding things from her. Besides, you didn't know her. She had a heart as big as a cathedral. She was the most forgiving person because she *understood*. I told her everything.'

Poor woman, thought the Marshal.

'And did you also tell her you would never leave her?'

'Of course I did. She knew that.'

Then she indeed had a cross to bear. Why did women do it? Why, instead of a strong man who would cherish them, did they marry men like this? Why couldn't they reserve their maternal instincts for their children?

'I'd like to talk to these women. Can you give me their names and addresses?'

'No, I can not! Look, are you trying to accuse me of something, or what?'

The Marshal, who was trying to do just that but failing, said not. He would find the women anyway. The funeral would produce Mary, and Mary would produce the others.

'Please do sit down,' he said, 'I didn't mean to upset you. Surely you understand that if someone dies in mysterious circumstances, and there's no obvious cause of death, we have to make inquiries.'

Forbes hovered a moment longer and then sat down in silence, his eyes fixed on the fire. The Marshal looked him over from head to foot. The clothes seemed to be the same except for the shirt. He had pushed up his sleeves to wash the cups and one of the shirt cuffs, dangling now below the rolled up brown sweater, was very frayed. The forearms were thinnish and very pale. He began rolling the sleeves down but stopped at one, distracted. Not a mark on him. The hands slim but with strong tendons. The Marshal imagined them pushing Celia Carter's head under the water even though we knew it couldn't have happened, not without a scratch on him.

Babies choke like that. They're helpless, can't lift their heads . . .
Why should Celia Carter be helpless?

Still watching the hands, he said, 'Your predecessor : . .'–

'Predecessor? What's that supposed to mean?'

'You just said your wife was married before. The child had a father, I imagine?'

'Oh, him. He's dead. He was old. Celia must have been looking for a father figure—Still, he had plenty of money so she did well out of it. She was a merry widow when I met her.'

'Then the child is alone in the world—or are there other relations?'

'She's not a child. There's no question of my having her here!'

'No, no . . . You'd hardly have room, of course. There's a house in London, you said?'

Again, Forbes folded his arms tightly. 'She's sure to get it. I live here.'

'Why?'

'Why what?'

'Why do you live here? Just my curiosity. I can't imagine suddenly leaving my own country and settling somewhere else—not,' he added, 'without good reason.'

'No, I don't suppose you could.' The implication was clear enough. The Marshal couldn't do it because he was an inferior sort of being, not of the right ambience, the one which allowed you to flit from country to country and in and out of other people's beds with your wife's consent. The Marshal insisted, 'Some problem, was there, that encouraged you to leave England?'

'No there wasn't any *problem*.'

'A relationship, then, that you wanted to get away from?'

'No! Have you never heard of people moving to Italy or

France because they like it? Because it's more civilized, especially artists and writers— Well, I suppose you don't meet many in your job.'

'Not a lot,' admitted the Marshal humbly, 'I expect that's what makes me so curious.'

And he was curious. More than that, he was unconvinced. It sounded all right, as it had when Signorina Müller had talked about the best architects in the world and all the rest of it. But he wasn't having it, not by a long chalk. If you're born and grow up in a country you belong there. And what about the language? And you don't have the same culture, the same feelings. You don't take all that on because of a few nice buildings. No, no, no, there has to be *a* reason. Italians who went to Germany went out of economic desperation and they couldn't get home fast enough. Emigrating was one thing, making yourself into an exile another. There'd be a reason, there had to be. You might have to dig for it, people might lie through their teeth about it, but it would be there. And he would find it. As he was reaching this decision he was saying, 'Of course, I know foreigners are fond of the paintings and architecture. Italy's a beautiful country. I come from Sicily, myself.'

'You're a long way from home, too, then.'

'Yes. Well, the army, you know . . .'

He could make a start by finding out whether Forbes had a criminal record in England. Not that he was very hopeful. Forbes looked the sort who left a lot of human wreckage behind him but always came out unscathed to get on with his life and his next article. But he would check.

And still the Marshal sat there, having asked all he could think of to ask, letting the other fill his increasing silences until it was one long silence on his side and Forbes was talking, talking, talking, trying to move, to convince, to make himself *liked*. But the Marshal only gazed at him with bulging, expressionless eyes, his body as still as Forbes's was agitated. When he thought he had been there long enough, he got up abruptly in the middle of one of Forbes's sentences. He didn't do it out of rudeness. The truth was that, as usual, he hadn't been listening to a word, only observing the increasing tension which he felt had now reached its limit. The man was very frightened. You could smell it in the room. So frightened that he couldn't even relax in relief at the Marshal's imminent departure. If he had done so, his relief would have been short-lived.

'I'll be back,' the Marshal announced, settling his hat, 'a bit later in the day.' This was true, though what he was thinking of doing was visiting Signorina Müller.

Forbes was rubbing a handkerchief between his palms which must have been sweating.

'You mean I'm supposed to stay in all day . . .'

'Oh . . .' The Marshal looked vague. 'Not if it puts you to any inconvenience.'

He felt sure that Forbes would stay in, would have stayed in anyway, even had he known his visit was to someone else, just so as not to miss anything. Well and good. He might think of something useful to ask him if he came back.

The Marshal did come back. His car was parked in the yard in full view of the little barn for a good hour and a half. The noise of its short-wave radio punctuated the quiet air with its sudden splutterings and its rasping, staccato messages. From behind the brick lattice-work, Forbes was undoubtedly watching and listening.

When the Marshal was ready to leave, the short winter afternoon was darkening. Automatically he buttoned his greatcoat and settled his hat as he approached the car and Fara started the engine. But he was surprised when he found himself feeling chilled. During the last hour or so, the temperature had dropped sharply. Looking across the Arno valley to his left, he saw the lights of Florence coming on beneath a stagnant burden of heavy clouds. But beyond that, where the lowering grey mass ended, the hills were sharply outlined against a horizon of ice-cold, purplish-blue daylight. And because the Villa Torrini was so quiet, you could hear it, a faint, far, distant moan.

CHAPTER 6

The *tramontana* reached Florence during the night, whipping red tiles from roofs, tumbling flower pots from their sills, slamming loose shutters against crumbling stucco. Television aerials were dragged free of their moorings to dangle precariously over the street, and rubbish bags from overspilling skips skittered along the roads until they burst and their contents whirled away to freedom. Mopeds crashed on to their sides to lie in the road and trees moaned and swayed as their weaker branches were torn off to destroy the cars parked in their shelter. By three in the morning the wind had roused just about every inhabitant of the city and sent them scurrying to bolt shutters, bring in forgotten laundry, rescue a favourite plant. When they had done all they could they lay awake because of the noise, sinister crashes that sounded too near for comfort, ambulance sirens, police sirens, fire engines. And when they got used to that they lay awake as the temperature plummeted below zero and tried to decide if they had the energy to get up again and fetch another blanket, or even turn up the heating which had been off for three warm, muggy weeks. Those who were managing to sleep through all this were woken very brusquely by their husbands or wives.

'Listen! Was that our roof?'

'Did you close all the shutters? Something's banging!'

'Are you asleep? Put your dressing-gown on and go and check—and while you're up . . .'

The Marshal, whose shutters were properly closed and whose heating was on, lay awake, nevertheless, listening to the noises outside. Not that they could be blamed for keeping him awake. He was listening to them because he already was awake and had been for some time. It was his own fault and he knew it. He was in agony. At supper he had kept dutifully to his diet which meant that, instead of dozing peacefully in front of the television, he had felt wakeful enough to study his notes on the new criminal procedures. He sat at the kitchen table to read so that Teresa could watch a film, and after about an hour and a half of it he was so gnawed by hunger that he found himself reading the same sentence five or six times without being able to take in a word. Full of righteous anger at being prevented from doing his duty, he made four sandwiches, chunky ones, from a fennel-flavoured sausage spiced with peppercorns. A fresh and fatty sausage which couldn't, with the best will in the world, be washed down with water. He washed it down with red wine.

For about half an hour he felt euphoric and read on with cheerful determination.

It is evident that the nature of these activities must be considered incompatible with the accusatorial role of the Public Prosecutor who must be on a plane of dialectical equality with the accused and can therefore have no powers of coercion over the latter and cannot assume a position of privilege in procedural terms.

All of which sounded reasonable enough while he was reading it but tended to evaporate as soon as he moved on. He took another run at it, shifting a little on the uncomfortable hard chair and absent-mindedly patting his stomach with one hand.

Consequent upon these considerations the new penal code provides for the elimination of the Judge of Instruction and a redefinition of the role of the Public Prosecutor . . .

It might be easier to concentrate in a better chair. He struggled on for a while before realizing just what was causing him so much discomfort. The four sandwiches seemed to have swollen into four loaves inside him. He must have overdone it. How could he have been so careless?

Well, there it was. By four in the morning the pepper-corns were burning holes in his insides and the irritation confounded itself with the turmoil outside and the problems churning round and round in his head. With all the ingredients of insomnia in place, he added the final touch that counts by starting to worry about how he would cope with appearing in court tomorrow if he got no sleep tonight.

Another siren . . . ambulance that one. He'd need one himself before long if he went on swelling. Perhaps if he got up and took something for the burning sensation, the movement might ease the situation. But he felt too tired and wretched to get out of bed. The ferocious howling of the wind distressed him like the noise of a crying child. He was filled with an undefined apprehension and was too tired to pinpoint its source, though he tried. After all, if he had to stay awake he might as well try and work a few things out. This exile business for a start. He hadn't been far wrong about that. Signorina Müller had left Austria during the war because her mother was Jewish . . . No, before the war, she'd said, seeing the way the wind was blowing, she'd gone to London. Then to a tiny seaside village to escape the bombing . . .

There was a crash and something metallic went bowling along on the gravel outside. There'd certainly be some damage to the trees in the Boboli Gardens.

He turned carefully on to his side in search of a comfortable position, but it was worse. He rolled on to his back again, always careful to try and avoid waking Teresa.

They'd threatened her with imprisonment as an enemy alien in England. It was true, what she'd said, that after an experience like that you're never at home anywhere, so you might as well choose whichever country you like best.

What about Forbes, though? She hadn't known of anything to his discredit but then, she didn't take that much interest in people. Couldn't blame her, after what she'd gone through, if she went in more for things than human beings. Less risky. If he did have a criminal record, the news would soon come through. System there was accusatorial . . . what was that part about the accusatorial role of the Public Prosecutor? *Must be on a plane of dialectical equality with the accused and therefore . . . and therefore . . . therefore what?*

He listened. That was the fire brigade. if only that wretched wind would die down a bit, but it would be three days. It always went on for three days. He had heartburn. If only he could get up the energy to go into the kitchen and make himself some camomile tea. Had he been asleep at all? He couldn't remember.

He did fall asleep for brief intervals, but the difference was slight. The wind still raged and the same thoughts fought with each other in his head and he was always aware of being in pain. Even so, there were things he could only be dreaming rather than thinking. At one point, Forbes had been showing him his forearms and explaining why they, and his hands, were free of scratches. The explanation had been convincing and the Marshal had even allowed himself to feel better disposed towards the man now that the mystery was cleared up. It was the wind, of course. He hadn't thought of that. How could anyone be expected to think with so much pain? He was doing his best. Therefore . . . the Prosecutor therefore . . . therefore . . .

'Salva!'

'What's to do?'

'You're talking to yourself. Are you all right?'

'I was asleep.'

He didn't want to tell her what the trouble was and have to start explaining about the sandwiches.

'You've been tossing about for hours.' She didn't ask any awkward questions but got up and went into the kitchen. He heard her put some water on to boil. He also heard her open the fridge and after a moment say, 'Oh, for goodness' sake . . .'

She brought him two tablets to chew and then a cup of camomile, not too hot. At about five-thirty he fell asleep.

'Professor Forli, you have described the injuries sustained by the deceased, Anna Maria Grazzini. Which of these injuries was the cause of death?'

'The internal haemorrhage caused by the blow which punctured the pancreas.'

'There is no question about that?'

'None whatever.'

'In your opinion, Professor, could Anna Maria Grazzini have recovered from these injuries had she received prompt medical attention?'

'It is possible.'

'Would you go so far as to say "probable"?'

'I think I could say that, yes. A blood transfusion would have saved her there and then. I can't, of course, say at this stage whether there might have been complications arising later from the head injuries but they were not so severe as to make it very likely.'

The Marshal had only just arrived and taken his seat. His face was burning, but as he looked around him he saw that almost everyone had the same problem. The freezing wind had whipped at their faces on the way here and now the courtroom was overheated.

'So, had the accused, on ceasing to inflict blows on the now virtually unconscious victim, decided to call an ambulance rather than reaching the decision they did reach, in your opinion Anna Maria Grazzini would be alive today?'

'With the reservation that other complications might have arisen, I'd say almost certainly.'

'And had the accused later followed the advice of the man answering their emergency call to the police and sent for an ambulance—then, even *then*, could she have lived?'

'That would depend on how much time had gone by, how much blood she'd lost in the meantime.'

'I can't tell you, Professor, how much blood she'd lost, but I can tell you that since they carried or dragged their bleeding, half-conscious victim down to a car and drove that car to a quiet lane behind the Belvedere Fort, that approximately fifteen to twenty minutes would have passed—assuming the times given us were correct.'

'In that case, it's less likely . . .'

'But still possible?'

'Perhaps, yes.'

'And yet, as we have heard, a *further ten minutes*—'

'Objection!' The defence counsel was on his feet. 'There is no possible way that my client could have known that Grazzini was suffering from an internal hæmorrhage. This line of questioning is tendentious in the extreme.'

'Objection sustained. The Prosecutor will confine himself to the facts as they presented themselves at the time. Hindsight is out of place in a courtroom.'

Quite right, too, thought the Marshal. Even so, the things he'd said, even if they were cancelled from the records, would have had their emotional effect. The defence was going for manslaughter and technically they might be right, but the Prosecutor was after a verdict of culpable homicide and would get it in all probability because of the way they'd dumped her. Dumped her, in the end, on himself.

'It is my contention,' boomed the Prosecutor, unabashed, 'that the three accused knew only too well that the injuries they had inflicted on Grazzini were serious. They knew they were serious because, otherwise, why did they try and dispose of her? Why not, if, as they say, her chief problem was her drunkenness, did they not simply—put her to bed! Leave her to sleep it off! Saverino Mario and Giorgetti Chiara had achieved what they wanted to achieve, had they not? They could now remove the child to their own home for Christmas. So why, ladies and gentlemen, did they not do just that? Why instead did they conceive an elaborate plan to get *rid* of Grazzini, to get her, and not the child, out of the flat? We have heard Saverino Mario say, "We didn't want her to die. We didn't want her to die and that's why we called the police." And that is proof, from the mouth of one of the accused persons, proof offered, not extracted, that they *knew*, ladies and gentlemen, they knew that her injuries were indeed grave. Grave enough for them to want to get rid of her. Grave enough for them to think that should she die and be found dead in that flat—'

'Objection!'

'Sustained. Mr Prosecutor, I hardly think your suppositions are relevant to the pathologist's evidence. Perhaps you would like to reserve them for your summing up. Defence.'

It was a relief for the Marshal to see that, though the Prosecutor was as aggressive as ever, he didn't use his repeating tactic on the pathologist. Perhaps it was a tactic unsuited to the authoritative witness and reserved only for the vulnerable and ignorant. Then he tried to decide where, between the extremes, he belonged.

That was Chiara Giorgetti's lawyer speaking. He needed to get a suspended sentence for her, no matter what the verdict, because of the little girl. It had been decided in the end that the child should not testify. That was something. She had been questioned and her answers recorded but had she been brought into court she could not, at ten years old, have failed to understand that she was testifying against her own mother in a murder trial.

The Marshal had visited the child twice in recent weeks. The grandmother had stopped sending her to school. There was trouble over that, but he could hardly blame her. The only answer would be to send her to a new school when all this was over.

Goodness, it was hot. Giorgetti's lawyer was short, fat and vociferous and his face was as red as a peony against his crooked white stock.

'Is it reasonable to suppose that Giorgetti Anna Maria—that Giorgetti Chiara, I beg your pardon—wanted merely to get rid of the injured woman? Why then did she—and it was she who decided—make that first phone call to the police? A phone call that could easily incriminate her, and which did incriminate her! She made that phone call on her own initiative and against the wishes of . . .'

Why the devil couldn't he manage to remember their names? The case had been going on long enough. Was he just a bad speaker or was he, too, floundering in the new system?

'Of . . . Saverino Mario. They were wrong. They were ignorant—ignorant of the consequences of their actions, and why? Because they had no way of knowing how serious the injuries to Grazzini were. Professor Forli, could a lay person possibly have known that an internal hæmorrhage was in progress?'

'I would doubt it.'

'There are no, shall we say, outward signs?'

'Oh yes—'

'But not such as a non-qualified person like Giorgetti Chiara, or even like myself, would be capable of interpreting?'

'I should say not, except—' the pathologist glanced at the judge and then decided to carry on: 'Except that in this case one of them had inflicted the damage, and a blow so violent to the abdominal region can hardly fail to have consequences.'

Very put out, but unable to find a comeback to this, the lawyer shuffled his notes unhappily and started trying to point out to the judge that the blow delivered was not in question since it had already been established that his client—whose name he managed to remember in time—had not been the one—

'Yes, yes. That's understood. May we get on?'

'No further questions.'

The Marshal was about to get to his feet but, after some whispered conversation, it seemed that Chiara Giorgetti was coming forward to speak for herself. Well, she could hardly do worse than her lawyer. As she seated herself on the red plastic chair she kept her eyes fixed on the judge. Two carabinieri positioned themselves behind her. Her black hair had grown long and straggly during her time in prison, but she certainly hadn't lost weight. She looked as bulky as ever under her red and green glittery wool sweater. She'd been wearing that when he arrested her, the Marshal remembered, or something very like it, dressed up for Christmas Eve.

'Giorgetti Chiara, what was your relationship with the deceased, Grazzini?'

It was the Prosecutor questioning her but she never looked at him, only at the judge.

'We weren't related . . .' Her loud voice tailed off as she realized just how loud it was with the microphone which her raucous tones hardly required. She made as if to shift away from it but didn't dare.

'I understand that there was no blood relationship. I want to know how you knew her, what part she played in your life, what sort of terms you were on.'

'She was living with Antonio.'

It was easy to see that she wasn't interested in the Prosecutor's questions. She answered them with the air of one brushing away a fly. Probably she had expected to be able to plead with the judge directly, to ask him to let her out of prison because of the child.

'She was living with Pecchioli Antonio, your ex-husband, is that correct?'

'Yes.'

'Did you leave your husband because of his relationship with Grazzini?'

'What? No. How could I? He didn't know her then. He met her after.'

'After you had left your husband and moved in with Saverino Mario whom you later married?'

'Yes.'

'The custody of your child was given to your husband?'

'Objection!' The lawyer's face was redder than ever as he jumped to his feet but he was overruled. The Marshal looked around the overheated room, watching faces, not listening. There was little he didn't know about Chiara whose mother, now looking after the little girl, had come to him years ago when she found out that her daughter was addicted to heroin. Not that she had found out, precisely, since she knew nothing of such things.

'*She told me, she screamed it in my face . . . I had nothing else to give her and she was shaking me, hitting me. Look at my eye. I'm ashamed to be seen in the shops and anyway, they won't give me any more credit. I've only my pension, you see, and though she goes missing for days at a time she's always there on pension day. She's always there . . .*'

Even after that, the poor woman had come into his office to report that her flat had been broken into and the television stolen. He'd had the job of gently dissuading her from reporting the theft and of getting Chiara into a community and off heroin. She'd stayed off it, too, largely because she'd got pregnant by Pecchioli almost immediately after coming out. Pecchioli, half her height and a quarter of her weight, so reminiscent of the Marshal's poor little friend Vittorio! But he'd kept them going. He had a job and he cared about the child. They'd been doing all right, keeping their heads above water, and after eight years of marriage they'd even got as far as leaving her mother's place for their own flat. It was dark and poky and the rent was disgracefully high, but even so ... And then along came Saverino and Chiara abandoned the kitchen sink and scraping along for a good time in the clubs and a few new clothes. She soon found herself back in the kitchen; this time with an occasional black eye to enliven the proceedings. The truth about the custody of the child was that the question had never legally come up. She stayed with her father because her mother had abandoned her, and her mother never gave the matter a thought until things started going badly, and she realized that she had nothing and no one. Saverino stayed around, provided she toed the line, but he was bored with her. It then occurred to Chiara that she missed her little Fiammetta who would at least have been company. Even then, she wasn't fool enough to apply for custody. Saverino had a record—not much of one, but a record nevertheless. Chiara had a history of drug abuse which her lawyer was now trying to prevent her revealing.

'Objection, Your Honour! Since the birth of this child ten years ago ...'

'Sustained.'

'Will you tell the court how the quarrel resulting in the death of Grazzini Anna Maria broke out?'

'It was Christmas Eve. Antonio had promised I could have Fiammetta for Christmas. Mario and me went to get her.'

'What time was this?'

'I don't know.'

'You don't know!'

There he went again. In this case, at least, there was some justification because she was lying, as the other two had, about what time the quarrel had broken out. The Prosecutor was right in assuming that they'd hardly have gone to pick the child up at midnight. Yet the woman had been dumped in the street in the early hours of the morning. The only reasonable conclusion was that they had waited hours before deciding they'd have to get rid of her. Hours when they knew how bad she was, otherwise they'd have gone about their business. But they didn't go, they stayed there, the three of them, with a woman bleeding to death on their hands, and the child . . . Hours of panic when, instead of sitting there paralysed, they could have saved her life and saved themselves from what was happening to them now. Why? Self-preservation, of course, was at the root of it, and had, in the end, been their undoing. If they hadn't tried to be clever . . .

And Forbes? He, too, had sat there, after whatever happened had happened, thinking, and as he thought he drank, to give himself courage. That had been his undoing. He'd drunk himself into a stupor.

'I'd done everything. I bought a crib and a tree with lights. Presents . . .' Chiara's voice broke and she was crying more than speaking when she said, 'I wanted my little girl! It was Christmas and I wanted . . .' She dashed the tears from her face and sniffed loudly, making the microphone splutter. 'I've no hanky . . .'

The little girl, Fiammetta, was the only one who might have told them what time her mother arrived with Saverino. But she hadn't told.

'*I can't remember. I think it was late.*'

And her eyes, in a face too old for her tiny body, had pleaded with the Marshal not to make her tell.

'*Do you want to live with your mum again?*'

'*Yes.*'

'*Aren't you happy living with your granny?*'

'*Yes.*'

'*And don't you want to stay with her?*'

'*Yes, but I can't.*'

'You can if you say you want to.'

'I can't. My mum said.'

'Why? Did she tell you why?'

'Because she's very old and she's going to die like Bobo.'

'Who's Bobo?'

'My granny's cat and he died because he was very old and he got run over, as well, and they put you in a box when you die and you can't come out because you have to stay at the cemetery so I have to live with my mum.'

Though her small face looked so old and drawn with misery, her mind was as underdeveloped as her body. When the Marshal had asked her if she could tell him about what happened she had drawn him a picture which, though she identified the stick figures for him, he didn't understand.

Later, a child psychiatrist had examined the drawing and the child, and recommended that she should not be subjected to the court hearing.

'Have you put my dad in prison or is he on his holidays?'

He hadn't been able to answer her but, in return for his having let her off, she let him off.

'Was Grazzini already drunk when you arrived—at whatever time it was?'

'She was already drunk and already making a scene.'

'Did she often do that?'

'Not all the time, but when she did she went crazy. Antonio tried to make her go to the doctor's but she wouldn't.'

'Why to a doctor? Because she was an alcoholic?'

'She wasn't an alcoholic, she was crackers. The drink always started her off but she was crackers and Antonio thought it was the accident. She got knocked off her moped by a fellow in a van and split her head open. It was after that that she started. She'd go to that piano bar in the piazza where they sing, and sooner or later she'd start quarrelling with somebody. If they threw her out she'd threaten to smash their windows and stuff like that. She'd scream abuse for hours and then start crying. They used to have to go for Antonio to come for her and he'd have such a time getting her home he'd be black and blue. She wasn't like that before the accident, but she wouldn't go to the doctor's anyway.'

'On the evening in question was she abusive or had she reached the crying stage?'

'She was screaming.'

'So she was abusive?'

'She was screaming and kicking out at Antonio. She didn't want him to let us take Fiammetta.'

'Did she say why?'

'She said the kid could stay in her own home for Christmas if it was good enough for the rest of the year.'

'And that was considered reason enough to start beating her?'

'Nobody started beating her! She was the one hitting out—and so that we couldn't take Fiammetta she'd hidden her clothes.'

'All her clothes?'

'The clothes she was supposed to wear. Stuff I'd bought her, a pink tracksuit that she'd set her heart on. It was supposed to be for Christmas, but I'd given it to Antonio so she could wear it to come out with us. That bitch had hidden it—or thrown it away. Anyway, we never found it.'

'Did you consider it unreasonable that after looking after your daughter all year, as indeed she had, there was some friction over her going to you at Christmas?'

'Christmas? What sort of Christmas was she going to get? There wasn't a card or a bit of tinsel up. The place was filthy and she hadn't even bought any food. That's why Antonio was on our side. How could he keep her there!'

'Nevertheless, I understand that these scenes which

occurred were not frequent and the fact remains that she did look after your daughter.'

'Look after her? Christ almighty, it was nine o'clock at night and the kid hadn't even had a meal!'

The Prosecutor relaxed and stood there in silence, letting it sink in. At first, it seemed as though Chiara was the only person in the room not to realize what she'd done. Then Saverino's voice hissed at her from behind the bars of his cage.

'Stupid cow!'

She whipped her head round in panic then, and seeing the Prosecutor's triumphant stance her face crumpled and she gave out a wail of fear.

Her lawyer, redder and more dishevelled than ever, requested permission to consult with his client and was granted it.

During the ensuing pause, the Marshal heard somebody come in and take a seat among the press. Galli from the *Nazione*. Not his style, this case, he usually went for bigger stuff. In fact there was already a *Nazione* reporter there, a much younger man. Galli was removing a long green loden overcoat. As always, he was immaculately dressed, and looked as though he'd just come from the hairdresser's. Quite possibly he had. Now what? He was making signs across the room, but there was no time to work out why because at that moment the Marshal was called.

He felt no apprehension as he seated himself in the red chair that was too small for him. The Prosecutor would no doubt delude himself into thinking, after the fact, that he had tricked that admission about the time out of Chiara when, in fact, his only intention had been to show her up as a bad mother and so remove any reason to deal lightly with her so as to reunite her with the child. The revelation had been entirely gratuitous and owed more to Chiara's bad temper than the Prosecutor's skill. As for the defence

. . . The Marshal, despite a slight, scratchy-eyed vagueness after his sleepless night, felt his strength, felt conscious of knowing all about Chiara and her family when the others had trouble remembering their names. He felt himself again. What's more, having put a stop to his diet by force after the sausage episode, Teresa had supervised his breakfast. If there was a connection between these facts, the Marshal was not conscious of it. He just felt better.

'Marshal, were you aware, before the events occurring on Christmas Eve, of the problems Pecchioli Antonio was having with Grazzini?'

'Yes. I'd been called out by the proprietors of the café she frequented.'

'Can you describe to the court what happened on that occasion?'

'Pozzi, the owner of the bar known as the Piano Bar in Piazza dei Cardatori number ten, telephoned to the Pitti station at seven twenty-five in the evening to report a disturbance. I went to the scene myself with carabiniere Di Nuccio and found Grazzini Anna Maria seated on the pavement outside the bar. A group of local people were standing around her, apparently trying to persuade her to go home.'

'Was she behaving in an aggressive manner?'

'Not when we arrived. She had broken a number of glasses and a chair inside the bar, but when we arrived she was crying loudly and accusing everyone of ill-treating her.'

'So in fact you never witnessed any violence on her part?'

'Oh yes. She gave carabiniere Di Nuccio a black eye and a number of bad scratches when he tried to pick her up.'

'And in your opinion, Marshal, can this truly be defined as aggressive behaviour or should it be more properly considered as the exuberance of a glass of wine too many?'

'It was neither.' He wouldn't be able to help it now.

'Neither?'

There he went! The Marshal's face didn't flicker.

'I understood from Pozzi that she arrived there perfectly sober and that he had only served her two drinks. Her behaviour was extremely bizarre and several witnesses testified to the fact that it dated back to the moped accident.'

'I see. However, you saw Grazzini, for whatever reason, behaving in a violent manner and were able to restrain her—the two of you, or just your carabiniere?'

'Just carabiniere Di Nuccio.'

'And was he forced to be violent in turn in order to restrain Grazzini? Did he handcuff her? Did he hit her? Throw her to the ground?'

'She was already on the ground. She flailed her arms at him when he bent to talk to her. He held her arms and got her to her feet. We then accompanied her home and gave her into the care of Pecchioli Antonio.'

'Thank you, Marshal. So, one man, without the use of violence, was able to deal with Grazzini when in an aggressive state. Can we come now to the twenty-fourth of December and hear what happened then?'

The Marshal wasn't too pleased with all this. Clearly, the presence of two large, uniformed men is going to have an effect that members of a family don't have. But he had no idea whether he was allowed to protest at this misdirection. He thought probably not. It wasn't his business—though the pathologist had got his in about their knowing they'd kicked her in the stomach . . . The moment passed and he could only carry on with his evidence.

'At 02.17 the bell at the Pitti Station was rung repeatedly. It was heard by my men whose dormitory is above the office where the bell rings. Two of the men went down to answer the housephone. A woman who refused to give her name claimed to have been passing through Piazza Pitti and to have seen someone collapse near our gate. When asked had she called an ambulance the woman said there was no phone near enough, and that all the bars were shut.

When my men arrived at the gates they found Grazzini Anna Maria lying on the ground. There was no sign of whoever had rung the bell. One of them called an ambulance and the other came for me.'

'Thank you, Marshal. Now, am I right in saying that during the night the Station at Pitti is closed and that all emergency matters are dealt with through your Headquarters at Borgo Ognissanti?'

'Yes. Anyone needing help can go there directly to report a crime or, if necessary, call out the emergency service on 112.'

'Yes. We know, in fact, that Giorgetti Chiara and Saverino Mario had already tried to call the police emergency number, 113. When that failed to produce what they wanted, instead of calling an ambulance directly as advised, and instead of calling the carabinieri emergency service on 112—they came and rang your bell! Do you have any idea why that should be?'

'Most probably because Giorgetti Chiara knew me. It often happens.'

'She knew you because you had helped her out of some— shall we say—difficulties, some years ago?'

Chiara's lawyer was almost on his feet. The Prosecutor veered away from this forbidden ground and the Marshal could see that it hurt him to do it.

'She didn't, however, want to see you, did she, Marshal? At that hour of night she knew your station was closed and you were in your bed. She didn't ask for you personally, and she certainly didn't wait around until you arrived. Isn't that true?'

'Yes.'

'So. Why you, Marshal, instead of 112? We have heard Saverino claim that it was, indeed, Giorgetti who insisted on going to Palazzo Pitti, claiming that you were the best person to deal with the matter. Wouldn't it be more logical to suppose that she rang your bell, knowing you were not on duty and knowing it would take you time to arrive, the time they needed to clear off the scene—in other words, a call to 112 might produce help too quickly from a nearby patrol and find them still in the vicinity!'

'Objection!'

'Sustained. Mr Prosecutor, the Marshal is not here to give opinions on your opinions but to give his evidence. May we please confine ourselves to the facts.'

'No further questions.'

'Counsel for the defence?'

Counsel for the defence, in an attempt to straighten his stock and his papers at the same time, sent the stock further askew and the papers fluttering to the floor. The Marshal waited, his bulging eyes expressionless.

'We have heard a lot of talk about violence, Marshal. You have known my client for some years, I believe. Would you say that she was a violent person?'

'No.'

'Do you consider her a strong person, a person who influenced the people and events around her?'

'No.'

'How would you describe her?'

'She was weak-willed, easily influenced.'

'Now, my client has stated that she took no part in the violence inflicted on Grazzini but was nevertheless unable to prevent it. Does that statement accord with your experience of my client?'

'Yes.'

'Do you consider it significant then that the weakest of the three people involved should be the one to insist on assigning to you, a person she knew to be trustworthy, the job of seeing that Grazzini was taken to hospital for treatment? That, given her weak character, this demonstrates very clearly her concern for Grazzini?'

'No.' It was all very well deciding to call her 'his client' to cover up that he kept forgetting her name, but he had prepared that little speech before Chiara had spilled the beans about the time. The Marshal didn't want Chiara to go to prison, but he shared the judge's opinion that they should stick to the facts and then decide. Fellow's face was getting even redder and you could see that he was going to insist because he had no alternative speech prepared.

'But is it not clear from her action, from her taking charge when before she had never taken charge, that of the three she was the one who cared?'

'Of the three she was the most frightened. She thought of me because I'd helped her out of a mess before.'

'That's only an opinion of yours, Marshal, if I may say so.'

'I beg your pardon. I understood that my opinion was what you asked for. She was frightened, though, that's a fact. When I went to the house she was hysterical. In any case she told me that she hadn't called 112 because it had occurred to her that they might be picked up before they got home. It's in her statement. She was afraid of that and of Grazzini dying, and she was afraid of losing Saverino.'

'Marshal, this is all yet more supposition, is it not?'

'No. It's in her statement.'

Furious, he changed the subject.

'Was Grazzini alive when you went out to the gate?'

'I wasn't sure . . . I thought so . . .' The Marshal paused, remembering his dream and expecting the Prosecutor to leap up and say 'You *thought*?' but the Prosecutor was deep in whispered consultation with his clerk.

'What action did you take?'

'I covered her with a blanket. She had a lot of injuries, so we didn't think we should move her. I tried to find a pulse.'

'She gave no sign of consciousness? Made no noise?'

'No, none. When the ambulance came I followed it to the hospital with one of my men. She was declared Dead on Arrival.'

'One last question. You know my client well, and consider her a weak character? Would you say that her behaviour depends largely on whose influence she is under?'

'Yes.'

'And would you describe the influence of Saverino as being a positive or a negative one?'

'Negative.'

Chiara wouldn't thank her lawyer for that. If he got her off at Saverino's expense there'd be a reckoning one day. They couldn't keep him in prison for ever.

'No further questions.'

'The court will adjourn.'

The Marshal was glad enough to rise from the uncomfortable little chair, but he had hoped that they might have got through the whole business whereas he was going to have to go through the arrest some other day. Oof! In the old days it was confirm your report and Good Day. He watched Chiara being led away and then made for the exit.

'Marshal!'

He smelled the perfume before spotting the person.

'Galli. I'm surprised you're bothering with this.'

'You're joking.' Galli slid into his dark green coat and felt tentatively at his bouffant black hair. He wasn't good-looking, carried too much weight, like the Marshal, but he looked as sleek and expensive as a pedigree cat and his wife, whom the Marshal had once glimpsed at some official do, was a real stunner. Long hair and long legs like a fashion model.

'I want to talk to you. Rang your office and they said you were here. It's about Forbes.'

CHAPTER 7

The Marshal buttoned his greatcoat and slid his glasses on before they reached the great baroque entrance where the dazzling sunlight would blind him.

'Five below zero last night,' Galli said. 'I think we lost a few tiles. That's going to cost me a packet.'

The carabinieri on guard looked frozen to the marrow, despite the extra thickness of their bullet-proof jackets. Clutching at their machine-guns, they hunched their shoulders against the agonizing blast of the *tramontana* which made their ears ring.

'Let me offer you a coffee.'

'Well . . . I've got my driver waiting.'

But Fara was as warm as toast, sheltered from the wind with the bright sun burning through the windscreen. They left him to wait a little longer. The Marshal had to hang tightly on to his hat as they crossed Piazza San Firenze and made for the welcoming warmth of a big bar near the corner.

They took their small thick coffee laced with a dash of grappa. The *tramontana* seemed to require it.

'It was Fusarri,' Galli explained, 'who told me you were on the Forbes case. He seemed as pleased as Punch about it.'

'Hmph.' That was another thing about Fusarri. He had friends among journalists where it was wiser to have just acquaintances. He and Galli probably went to the same tailor and hairdresser. They both smoked too much. Galli was lighting up now, but a normal cigarette, thank God.

'You don't like him? I suppose he's not your sort. Still,

you people never like any magistrate as a matter of principle, admit it.'

The Marshal, as a matter of principle, admitted no such thing.

'I just find him odd, that's all. That way he has of looking as if he's got more important things on his mind and is only listening to you out of politeness. I know he's kept busy, but, after all, what can be that much more important than the case he's on?'

'Women.'

'What?'

Galli chuckled delightedly.

'You didn't know that? Well, I suppose he wouldn't be likely to chat to you about it. They're his only real interest, apart from food and smoking. Quite a swordsman, too, I can tell you. We've had one or two girls in common—not at the same time, he's not a man I'd care to offend.' Galli grinned sideways at the Marshal, squinting against a curl of smoke. 'Trust you, Guarnaccia, to get his number. He *is* only listening to you out of politeness—well, out of a sort of informed interest, as you might say. He could easily afford not to work but he enjoys it.'

'Mph. That explains a lot.'

'Up to a point it does, but don't get the wrong idea. He's brilliant. Anyway, tell me about Forbes. You going to arrest him?'

'Why? I wouldn't have thought there was much in it for you.'

'There isn't, if you mean a story. I'm on the Bribe City job full time. I'm interested in Forbes because the Forbeses are friends of ours, have been for years.'

'In that case,' the Marshal sighed, 'you can tell me more than I can tell you. What I can tell you, given that you're not writing it up, is that I'm not the person who should be on the case. My business is with people like them.' He indicated the Tribunal opposite. 'Something like that happens and I can have the culprits inside in a few days. This Forbes chap . . .'

'You don't like him? Forget I asked. You don't or you'd answer. Well, having said we're friends . . .' Galli hesitated.

'It was her you liked,' finished the Marshal.

'Then you do know something?'

'No, no . . . Just one of her neighbours chatting. She said it was something they quarrelled about, Forbes and his wife, that all their friends were her friends really.'

'I suppose that's more or less true. No, I thought you might have found out—you will anyway, it's common knowledge—that I had a bit of a thing for her myself.'

'No, I hadn't found out. You were lovers?'

'We would have been if I'd had my way but she was ferociously loyal. She fancied me, though I say it myself, but she wouldn't, she said, not until she'd definitely given up on Forbes, a thing she was loath to do. Nobody likes admitting they've picked a lemon, do they? At least, women don't. They think it makes them look fools or failures. Well, he was the one who was a fool and a failure. Not that he could help being a failure, but he could help being a fool. Fancy having a woman like that—she was one in a million, I can tell you—and leaving her without. He hadn't touched her in a year, she told me that. Anyway, whoever said that about their friends wasn't far wrong. I think he's a right little turd, pardon the expression, and if he had something to do with her death I'm interested, story or no story. What do you need to know?'

'I wish I even knew that. This Forbes . . . He'll inherit a goodish bit, I gather.'

'Mm.' Galli looked unconvinced. 'Two more coffees,' he told the barman. 'If you're talking about a motive, I can't

see that being it. He had full use of her money as it was,
without the responsibility of it.'

'Didn't he earn anything at all?'

'Him?' Galli laughed. 'How would he ever earn
anything?'

'He says he's writing an article.'

'Oh, he's always writing an article. Might even have been
paid for one or two of them but they're the ones Celia'd
been asked to write and given to him. Probably did half
the work herself, anyway, and gave him the credit. The
others he does for nothing, for some English language
magazine that's printed here and given away free by hotels.
The rest of the time he works on his mythical book. No, he
doesn't earn anything, but she gave him all the money he
wanted.'

'Like a spoilt child, by the sound of it.'

'That's what he is. And when she wasn't writing the
articles for him, he'd be round at my office or at Mary's to
try and get one of us to provide.'

'And did you?'

'More or less. Difficult to get out of it. Among journalists—real journalists—it's done. We give each other a hand
since we're always pushed for time. But it's reciprocal. Not
like with Forbes.'

The Marshal frowned and accepted a second coffee. The
bar was filling up with people taking their morning break.

'You're not in competition, then?'

'Certainly not with jerks like Forbes! No. I know what
you mean, but there's no competition to get the story out
before the other papers, not when it's been on the TV news
the night before.'

'I suppose not. Still . . . he struck me as an intelligent
man, even so—not that I'm a judge.'

'Oh, he's intelligent enough, but he'll never make a journalist or a writer of any sort. Doesn't communicate. He's

only interested in himself, you must have noticed that—
Will you excuse me a minute?'

The young journalist who had been in court had come
into the bar and was signalling for a word with Galli. They
stood together near the door, talking rapidly under their
breath, while the Marshal stayed near the counter, gazing
tranquilly through its glass at the heaps of cream cakes and
plates of fresh sandwiches. The thought of a real lunch
awaiting him at the end of the morning left him feeling
calm.

'Sorry.' Galli returned with an unlit cigarette dangling.
'Mario's the one who's following the Forbes case, by the
way.' The young journalist was still in the bar but didn't
approach them. 'Wrote the story about Julian being found
blind drunk in the bedroom. Is that true?'

'Yes, it's true.'

'He wanted to talk to you, but I put him off.' Galli
removed his cigarette, looked at it speculatively, and put it
back in his mouth.

'I'm afraid I don't have a light . . .' the Marshal said.

'No, I don't want a light. I'm trying to give up so I don't
light them for a bit. What were we saying?'

'About Forbes only being interested in himself. But by
his own account he was interested in women. This Mary,
for instance, among others.'

'*What?* Forbes? Who told you that?' Galli unstuck the
cigarette from his lip and held it between forefinger and
thumb as he stared at the Marshal in amazement.

'He did,' the Marshal said. 'He was talking about a
number of women though he only gave me the one name.
After all, if he and his wife weren't—'

'God, what a bastard. It's not true, any of it. He's off his
head! Mary barely tolerates him and that only because
she's—was—a close friend of Celia's. And if he really was
having it off with anybody else, you can bet your life we'd

all know about it. You can't keep a secret like that in a town this size—Oh, I've seen him trying, many a time, but I've never seen him succeed. What a filthy trick to say a thing like that about Mary, and to you.'

'Perhaps not only to me. He claims he told his wife.'

Galli was as appalled as the Marshal had been.

'In that case maybe she'd at last decided to leave him and there's your motive.'

'Very nice. Except that he told me about it. You've seen him trying to pick up women, you said. Where would that be?'

'At Il Caffè. Two or three nights a week. We all go there.'

'What café?'

'Il Caffè. You must know it, it's right across from your station in Piazza Pitti.'

'Oh, that place. It stays open too late.'

'It stays open until a decent hour for people like us who sometimes work till eleven or even midnight. And if you want to know something else he's been going there this week, after Celia's death. And she's not even in her grave yet.'

The Marshal, who had always seen Galli as cynical in the extreme, looked at him in surprise. He was upset.

'You really cared for her?'

'Yes, I did.' He put the cigarette in his mouth and lit it quickly. 'She must have told somebody. If she was going to leave him she'd have told somebody. Talk to Mary. She's the most likely one—and ask her about Christmas. Whatever he did, or told her he'd done, it must have been at Christmas.'

'Why do you say that?'

'Because nobody saw them. They didn't turn up to any parties when they'd said they would. We all knew something was up.'

The Marshal sighed. 'Well, I'll ask. I hope she can tell me something because I got nothing out of him. Except, when I think about it, that he bought her some furniture.'

'*He* bought?'

'Well, yes, after what you've said I suppose it must have been with her money, but it's not much help all the same, is it?'

He looked out through the doorway at the steps to the Tribunal across the square. 'I'm grateful to you for what you've told me, but I still wish . . . I arrested those three the day after it happened. I've known Chiara Giorgetti since she was a teenager, and I know her mother.'

Galli followed his glance. After a moment's silence he said, 'You've done it before—if that's what you mean, if you're bothered by their being foreigners. There was that Dutch business—'

'No, no . . . it's not just that. The Dutchman, he was an artisan, not a writer, not an intellectual, and besides, I never spoke to any of those people. You may not think much of Julian Forbes, but he's cleverer than I am and I know nothing about him. I don't understand him and I never will. Still, it's not your problem. I don't know why I'm saying these things to you.'

'Because I cared about her, that's why, isn't it?'

'It might be, I suppose.'

'Well, whatever the reason, it's not true, what you're saying. Julian Forbes is a coward, morally and physically. You probably scare the living daylights out of him. And, whatever you may imagine about intellectuals, forget it. What's the difference? Sex, drink, jealousy, panic and cowardice. All the world's a village; it'll take you a bit longer to get Forbes but there's no rush, is there? As long as you get him before he damages anybody else the way he damaged Celia. She deserved better, and now it's too late.'

'Out of the depths have I cried unto Thee, Oh Lord. Lord, hear my voice. Let Thine ears be attentive to the voice of my supplication.'

The Marshal had placed himself right at the back of the little church so as to leave a number of pews between himself and Celia Carter's family and friends. The mass had already begun when he slipped in. The priest, who was Irish, had said the mass in Latin, since there were people from various countries present, but the prayers he was saying now, as he blessed the coffin, were in English. It was all so unexpected, but then everything that he had learned since yesterday evening when Father Jameson had got in touch with him had been unexpected. The first surprise had been that she was a Catholic.

He'd assumed that, being English, she would belong to the English church. He'd thought to find himself at a Protestant service in Via Maggio, instead of which he was in the little church belonging to the hospital of San Giovanni di Dio, almost next door to carabinieri headquarters in Borgo Ognissanti. Father Jameson had explained that he said mass there in English once a week. Not that Celia Carter had ever attended. He had met her just the once, he said, but when Mary Price Mancini, her close friend and a practising Catholic, had come to organize the funeral, he had decided to speak to someone. He had visited headquarters in search of whoever was in charge, and had eventually been taken to the office of Captain Maestrangelo, who had listened to him and then telephoned the Marshal.

'A Jesuit, Irish, though he's been here most of his life. I think you should hear what he has to say.'

'She was a Catholic? I never thought . . .'

'No, I was surprised myself. In any case she didn't go to church, so . . . You couldn't come over here to the church? They're bringing the body in this evening and he wants to be there.'

'Of course.' And he had gone. The coffin already lay then, as it lay now, in the aisle before the altar. The priest had been kneeling beside it at the end of the pew on the left, praying as he was praying now. The prayer had been in Latin then and the Marshal had understood it. In English he could only pick out the odd word, but he had served at enough requiem masses as a child to know that it was the same.

'*If Thou, Oh Lord, shalt observe iniquities, Lord, who shall endure it?*'

Hat in hand, he had made his genuflection, waited a moment, then touched the priest on the shoulder.

'Ah . . . Is it you? It's so dark in here and my eyes aren't what they were.'

There were just the two candles lit at the head and foot of the coffin. The Marshal had barely been able to distinguish the altar where a bunch of wax white lilies perfumed the chilly air. Their scent was covered now by that of the incense as Father Jameson circled the coffin. He moved slowly with an almost imperceptible limp.

'*For with Thee there is merciful forgiveness and by reason of Thy law I have waited for Thee, O Lord.*'

There were a great many candles lit this morning, so that the altar at least was illuminated. The small door into the sacristy, though, was still hidden in gloom.

Father Jameson, last night, had gone through first, the Marshal following.

'You must mind the step. I hope you won't feel too cold with just the one bar. I try not to use too much electricity here, my parishioners not being rich. You do understand . . . At one time I said the English mass and heard confessions in the cathedral, but this is very good. We're quiet here and we have our Sunday mass now. Sit down, Marshal—forgive me, I don't remember your name though you told me.'

'Guarnaccia.'

'Guarnaccia. Yes, yes. Marshal Guarnaccia—not a Florentine name?'

'No, I'm from Sicily.'

'Ah. I was never there but I think it must be very beautiful, especially the sea. The "wine-dark sea"—I'm thinking not of Homer but of the story by Sciascia, your fellow Sicilian, a fine writer. Warm your hands a little, they're blue with cold.'

The Marshal did so gratefully. They were frozen despite his heavy leather gloves.

'Thank you. It's a fierce wind.'

'It is indeed and it chills the bones and my bones are old and a bit rheumatic. I think the good Lord will forgive us if we drink a drop of Marsala, do you think so?'

He took the bottle and two small glasses from a tall, antique cupboard. The Marshal's chair was also antique, as big as a throne and elaborately carved. But the other chair was a kitchen chair, made of Formica or something similar, and the table, though shrouded in worn tapestry, undoubtedly went with it, judging from the just visible straight metal legs. The one bar electric fire looked old and cheap, and the priest's black trousers shone with age. Yet there was something about Father Jameson that made all this irrelevant. The Marshal liked him. He felt comfortable with him, and even before the priest had told him what he had to tell him, he felt for the first time that here was somebody who would take away some of the burden of this business.

'*My soul hath relied on his word: my soul hath hoped in the Lord.*'

Apart from anything else, he had been of practical help, telephoning to Mary Mancini himself to arrange for her to meet the Marshal this morning after the funeral. The Marshal was pretty sure that he could guess which one she was even from behind. She would be the one standing next to the thin fair girl who must be Celia Carter's daughter. With what he knew now, he would certainly have to talk to the girl at length, but he would be happier doing that after a word with Mary, who might, he hoped, know what it all meant.

The church was so cold there must be no heating on at all. If those lilies had been carved in ice they wouldn't have melted. The Marshal's ears and nose were frozen.

'From the morning watch even until night let Israel hope in the Lord.
'Because with the Lord there is mercy . . .'

In general, he was inclined to agree with Signora Torrini about priests. But then, his experience had been mostly of the country village priests down home, the sort who warned you that your soul would turn black and suppurate if you didn't take Holy Communion . . . Why had she brought that up, anyway? He ought to remember to ask her. In any case there was something about Father Jameson that had made him feel better last night, made him sit peacefully sipping his tiny glass of Marsala, in no hurry to come to the argument in question, despite the chill that the one bar fire did so little to dispel. They had talked for a while of their respective homes and it was the Marshal who first mentioned the subject of exile.

'Well now, Marshal, no priest from anywhere in the world would consider himself in exile in Italy, the home and heart of the Church. And there's some truth in that perhaps as regards any Catholic.'

'You mean someone like Celia Carter? But I understood she wasn't a practising Catholic.'

'No. But perhaps that's not quite what I meant. I'm thinking more of questions of culture, of education. The good Mary Mancini, now, she's comfortable here, married to an Italian, more so than she might be married to an Englishman of the Protestant faith. Of course, since Vatican

II there have been great changes and mixed marriages are
not frowned upon so much as they were. Nevertheless, they
create problems and, in my experience, they've never been
problems that were, so to speak, clearly defined religious
ones. They're subtle and persistent problems of very different sensibilities which, even in these days of Ecumenicism,
show no signs of resolving themselves.'

'And Celia Carter suffered, you think, from problems like
that?'

'I'm certain of it.'

'Is that why she came to see you?'

'Oh, she didn't come to see me, Marshal, no.'

'I understood from Captain Maestrangelo . . .'

'That I'd talked to her. Yes, indeed I did. But she didn't
come looking for me, though she was certainly looking for
help. I didn't go into detail with your Captain. No doubt
he's a busy man and besides, he felt you were the person
who should be told. No, she didn't come here at all. You
might say I found her or that she found me. I don't know.
It was in the cathedral after Saturday mass at which I'd
served, as I sometimes do during busy festive periods.'

'Was this around Christmas time?'

'You already know something about it, then?'

'Not really. Only that something went very wrong and
that it happened around Christmas.'

'I see. Yes. You're right. It was Christmas Eve. I served
at the normal Saturday mass so that those who usually did
so could rest before serving at midnight mass. I was going
home. It would be about six o'clock, I would think, and
there were few lights on in the cathedral and very few people
remaining. Just a small group lighting candles at the crib
and another with guide books looking at the fresco of John
Hawkwood.

'I didn't notice her at once, and when I did it was only
as a dark shape out of the corner of my eye, and I imagined

she was one of those elderly women who often kneel alone
in empty churches to pray. Then, for some reason, I looked
at her more carefully. There was something wrong, something about the figure that was too rigid. I had almost
passed by her but I stopped. She wasn't praying, not then.
She was kneeling, but she looked more as though she'd
collapsed. Her arms were hanging limply by her sides and
some shopping, Christmas shopping, had tumbled to the
floor. Her eyes were closed, she was breathing very slowly
and deeply. I touched her shoulder, afraid she was ill.

' "Are you all right? Do you need help?"

'She turned her face towards me and I realized that the
deep distressed breathing was in fact a form of weeping.
Her cheeks were wet with tears and her eyes were very
swollen. She spoke to me in Italian.

' "I can't go home . . ."

' "Indeed you can't, in such a state. Sit down now, a
moment."

'I had to help her and, to be honest, despite her evident
grief, I was worried that her health was compromised, that
she might suffer a serious physical collapse.

' "Do you feel faint?"

'She shook her head. "I can't go home." She made an
effort at collecting her Christmas parcels but her fumbling
only caused them to tumble about more and the very sight
of them seemed to distress her. She pushed them away from
herself and began sobbing. We all, even as small children,
cry in a different way when somebody can hear us, did you
ever notice that, Marshal? I collected the parcels together
and took her arm.

' "Come with me now a moment and sit quietly until
you're feeling better. It's so cold in this great place."

'She came with me quite docilely, and yet I felt she had
little enough strength to walk and I had to support her. I
could feel the physical weight of her grief. I sat her down

in one of the sacristan's rooms and switched on the light.

'"Is there anything I can offer you?"

'She shook her head. I was still worried that she might collapse. It was clearly a great effort for her to breathe.

'"Do you want to tell me about it? Is it something you want to confess?"

'She looked at me blankly. "Confess?"

'"You are a Catholic?"

'"I suppose so, yes. But I don't go to church . . ."

'"You came today. Were you at Holy Mass?"

'"No . . ."

'I sat down before her. She looked as though she might fall forward. She was still crying, but the tears rolled steadily down her cheeks in silence now, and she seemed unaware of them.

'"Try to breathe more deeply. That's it. You're very distressed. Look at me, child. I'm a priest and I'm also a very old man. Whatever it is I've probably heard it before, and it might give you some relief to tell someone, a stranger especially, if you prefer to think of me so, rather than as a priest."

'"Yes."

'"Have you told no one at all what's troubling you?"

'She shook her head. "I'm ashamed, I can't . . ."

'"But there's nothing you want to confess?"

'She shook her head. "I don't know what I've done . . . But there must be something I did or should have done. I feel responsible but there's nothing to confess."

'"What made you come into the cathedral, do you know?"

'"Oh yes. I was frightened."

'"You need help."

'"I was frightened. I was trying so hard and I thought . . . I was managing, shopping. I bought things. I bought— then I just collapsed inside. I can't cope, I can't! And I

don't want to die, Father, you must believe that, but perhaps that's how it happens, against your will!"

'"Suicide?"

'"Yes.."

'"That's what you're afraid of?"

'She nodded. "But I don't want it. Believe me."

'"I do believe you, child. Will you pray with me for a
moment?"

'"I can't, not in words."

'"Well, well. Your being here is a prayer in itself, isn't
it? Did you pray as a child?"

'"With my father, when I was very small."

'"And what prayer did you say together? Do you remember one after all these years?"

'"Only one. *Out of the depths . . . have I cried to Thee . . .*"

'"The *De profundis?*" It seemed a strange choice for a
young child. "It's very beautiful. A penitential psalm. Will
we say it together now?"

'"I can't remember very much . . ."

'"*Out of the depths have I cried unto Thee, O Lord:*
'*Lord, hear my voice.*
'*Let Thine ears be attentive to the voice of my supplication.*
'*If Thou, O Lord, shalt observe iniquities, Lord, who shall endure
it?*
'*For with Thee there is merciful forgiveness and by reason of Thy
law I have waited for Thee, O Lord.*
'*My soul hath relied on his word: my soul hath hoped in the Lord.*
'*From the morning watch even until night let Israel hope in the
Lord.*
'*For with the Lord there is mercy and with him plentiful
redemption.*
'*And He shall redeem Israel from all his iniquities.*"

'As I finished the prayer I saw that she had begun

to breathe properly and her colour was slightly better.

'"I hadn't forgotten it. I thought I had, but I remembered each phrase as you said it. Thank you. He was such a good man, my father. Do you think it really means anything, the phrase they always use—while the balance of his mind was disturbed?"

'She told me then, and I understood what she was afraid of. She was afraid of grief, of unbearable grief of the sort that had ended in her father's suicide. She told me all about her mother's illness—she'd have been no more than eight or nine years old herself then—a terrible form of cancer which disfigured her face so that near the end she refused to let the child see her.

'"She didn't want to frighten me. She didn't want to be remembered like that."

'She knew, as children do know things, that her father had somehow helped her mother to die.

'"Did I listen to those whispered conversations between him and his sister? I can't honestly remember. I never saw the morphine suppositories that the nurse left each day and yet I was aware of their presence and the feeling of dread that they provoked, a cold sick panic in my stomach."

'Her father had outlived his wife by less than a year.

'"He did it with sleeping pills. They say that's a woman's suicide but he put a plastic bag over his head to make sure."

'She was too young to help him, too young to talk to him, but sensitive enough to feel inadequate and to take the blame.

'"It wasn't just because he missed her, I'm sure of that. He must have been lonely, but the horror of her illness coupled with his guilt about the morphine . . . Oh, I don't blame him in any way, not now."

'"But you blame yourself?"

'"I couldn't help him. I wasn't strong enough. I wasn't important enough."

'"You were only a child."

'"It doesn't matter! Age has nothing to do with it. I didn't help him. Do you know, everything I do, every book I publish, every good review, every success, it's all to make it up to him, to console him, to give him something to live for—only he's dead. What sense does it make? I've never told anyone this before, and maybe I didn't even know it until just now when I said it. I think that's why I don't like living in England where I might think about it."

'"But something provoked you into thinking about it. Your own grief which makes you fear suicide, which you think might overwhelm you?"

'"Yes, that . . . *Out of the depths have I cried unto Thee, O Lord: Lord, hear my voice*—but he didn't! My father was a good man."

'"But you're very angry with him, is that not so?"

'"Angry?"

'"He deserted you. It doesn't seem to me that you've forgiven him. Now you're angry with me, are you not? But suicide is a very big sin for such a small child to forgive. Perhaps you should have left it to God."

'"Aren't we meant to forgive each other?"

'"Oh yes, but we're such amateurs, don't you think? And God's a professional—ah, you can smile, then? I'm glad of that. Wait, now, while I switch on this lamp, that's a sad little light bulb up there and I can hardly see you."

'I had to see her. After all, she was only telling me of things that happened many years ago. Important things but not the things that had brought her into an empty cathedral on Christmas Eve. I watched her face as I spoke.

'"Christmas can be such a difficult time. For the poor, for the lonely, for the newly bereaved."

'She didn't answer but she closed her eyes for a moment and she was surely close to tears again.

'"It's very tiring to talk of things which affect us deeply. Perhaps you should go home now. I'm always ready to listen if you want to come and talk again."

'She shook her head.

'"I *did* forgive him! How could I not forgive him when he went through so much? And I swore I'd never let anyone I loved down again, never desert them in their hour of need! But it doesn't work, and I don't know what more I can do!"

'"No, indeed. You're doing a great deal too much and all to comfort yourself. You were the one deserted, poor creature, abandoned in your hour of need. And aren't you manipulating others to ease your own pain?"

'I wonder now was I too cruel, too sudden—but, of course, I was thinking I might never see her again, as indeed I didn't. She was an intelligent woman, too, otherwise I wouldn't have taken such a risk. It's such a common problem, Marshal, don't you think, the way we console ourselves through others? Most people use their children, have you noticed that ever? Do you have children yourself?'

'Two boys.' The Marshal felt a faint wave of apprehension, an anticipation of some unacknowledged guilt.

'Two little boys.' The priest's eyes gleamed, not with accusation but with kindliness. 'They must have been hard times when you were young in Sicily, as they were when I was young in Ireland.'

'They were.' His tone was defensive.

'And you must get a great deal of pleasure out of giving them all the things you once lacked.'

The Marshal thought of their skiing holiday, and a number of little luxuries which he knew he shouldn't have

given in to, but which he'd been proud to be able to afford.
Did he spoil them?

'You spoil them a little. It's a small selfishness, Marshal,
but because of it they won't have your strength of
character.'

'It's hard to refuse them what you can afford to give
them.'

'True. It's very hard—and then, if we did, they might
well misunderstand and resent it. There's no simple answer.
In any case, that Christmas Eve I took the risk of at least
posing the problem and she understood me, I'm quite sure
of that. Now, when I heard you were investigating her
death, I felt at once that I should talk to you. I felt as sure
as human fallibility allows, that she didn't commit suicide,
that whatever her problem was, she left here more clear in
her mind and with a crisis behind her. It also occurred to
me, though I'm trespassing here on your territory perhaps,
that someone who knew how close she'd come to the idea of
suicide . . . Well, perhaps I shouldn't take the liberty . . .'

'Might have tried to make it look that way?'

'I suppose something of the sort, yes. But, of course, I
don't know all the circumstances of her death.'

'No one does.' The Marshal frowned. 'There's certainly
no evidence to suggest suicide. On the other hand, unless
I can find out what happened at Christmas . . .'

'True. But, as I said, Christmas tends to bring things to
the surface, precipitate a crisis. It could have been going
on for some time, this problem.'

'Yes . . .' The Marshal toyed with the idea of telling him
about the Mary Mancini business. He wouldn't take too
kindly to the idea, probably. She seemed to be one of his
best parishioners and, in any case, it looked as though the
story was untrue. He decided to be vague.

'It could be there was some other women—Forbes told

me so himself, her husband—and it may well be that he told her about it at Christmas.'

The old priest didn't speak for a moment or two. He looked down at the tiny glass and turned it slowly between his dry fingers. 'Yes, well . . . that's something that would cause very great distress, of course . . .'

'But not so much distress as she was feeling?'

'I'm sure that wasn't it. No, no. No, Marshal, that wasn't it at all. Do you remember that she told me she felt ashamed? But it wasn't she who had strayed because she had nothing, she felt, to confess. No, it was something worse than that. Seeing how exhausted she was, I gathered her parcels together and helped her up.

'Walking back down the aisle of the cathedral I could sense her reluctance to face the world outside. She was dragging her steps. The organist had begun practising for midnight mass, playing something, I don't remember now just what, from *The Messiah*, and it brought a phrase to my mind—you'll remember it—*A man of sorrows, and acquainted with grief* . . .'

'Celia, God rest her soul, was acquainted with grief. But it was her daughter, Marshal, who was at the root of it. In fact, until I spoke of it to Mary Price Mancini this morning, I remained under the impression that the child was dead, perhaps drugs, something of that nature.

'We reached the doors at last and I tried to give her the parcels. She broke down again. She couldn't bear to touch them—that was why I thought the child was dead, you see.

'"I bought her everything . . . I bought—things she wanted, everything I could think of that she—Oh God, I don't want to go home!"

'She pulled herself together as best she could but she wouldn't touch the parcels. She insisted I kept them and gave them to any parishioners I thought had need of some

Christmas cheer. She tried to laugh, as though she were trying to ridicule herself. "I even bought a tree . . ." But she was weeping. The last thing she said was, "I want my little girl! Anything else I could bear but not this. I want my little girl!"

'She pushed her way out of the side door and it swung to behind her. I followed as best I could on my rheumatic legs, but when I came out to the top of the cathedral steps she had disappeared among the crowd of Christmas shoppers. There it all was, the bustle and cheerfulness, the dark afternoon glittering with Christmas lights, and somewhere among all this a good woman whose name I didn't know, and whose heart was acquainted with grief.

'We can do so little for each other, Marshal, so very little. Well, well, I prayed with her that Christmas Eve and tonight I'll pray beside her. She won't be alone. That's why I asked you to come to me here, though it was a hard thing to drag you out on such a night.'

'No, no . . .' the Marshal said, standing up stiffly in the cold little room. 'No, you did quite right.'

CHAPTER 8

'Eternal rest give unto her, O Lord,
'And let perpetual light shine upon her.
'May she rest in peace.'

The Marshal slipped out quietly and waited near the door, sheltering himself as best he could from the freezing wind. He watched as Forbes followed the coffin out. He wore some sort of darkish suit, though it wasn't black and neither was his tie. The daughter walked out beside him and he got his first look at her face. She was pretty. Very delicate and fragile-looking, rather fairer than her mother. She wasn't dressed in black either, but wore a heavy, dark bluish sort of coat. She glanced at the Marshal, not so much by accident, he thought, but as though she were seeking him out. He was surprised by the darkness of her eyes which you would have expected to be blue with such light hair. She had pink lipstick on. She looked, thought the Marshal, though he didn't consider himself much of an expert, very pretty indeed. When they started loading the coffin into the hearse, she faltered and made as if to support herself on Forbes's arm, but he anticipated her movement and slid sideways away from her. Mary Mancini moved forward quickly and took the girl's arm, steering her gently into the car behind. Forbes got in at the other side but it was evident that this was only because there was the one hired funeral car available, everyone else having their own transport. He sat close to the far window, looking out, and never once had he acknowledged the Marshal's presence. Even so, he might have had eyes in the back of his head, so strong was the Marshal's impression that he was aware of no one else.

'Shall we go?' Mary Mancini was beside the Marshal. She spoke in a whisper. She'd told him earlier that she didn't intend to go to the cemetery because her youngest child would be home from school before they got away if she did.

The funeral cortège departed and they crossed the road behind it.

'Is that your car and driver? We might as well go on foot, you know. We're just across the bridge here and it's bound to be quicker.'

The Marshal was frozen to the marrow but could hardly contradict her. He paused to instruct Fara and then they set out across the bridge. It was difficult enough to breathe in the face of such a wind but Mary Mancini seemed to find it stimulated conversation.

'He's a good-looking boy, isn't he?'

'I'm sorry . . . ?'

'Your driver. He looks very bright, too, and he obviously worships you!'

A remark like that, plus the wind, deprived the Marshal of speech and they crossed the bridge in silence.

'Left here. Don't you just love the *tramontana*? I always think of it as a sort of spring cleaning. The Arno valley's so stagnant as a rule, it's like breathing armpit. This is just what we need.' She held up her face and breathed in the icy air with delight. 'Of course, what we don't want is a lump of exquisite renaissance architecture thundering down on our heads.' A remark inspired by the presence of the fire brigade who had closed the street they were trying to enter in the hope of preventing just that contingency. 'We can cut through here.'

Her street was a quiet backwater where the ground floor shops were occupied almost entirely by artisans. Today, apart from a prevailing smell of glue and varnish, they weren't much in evidence, their doors shut fast against the wind so that the usual sounds of sawing and sewing and the music from their radios were barely audible. There was just one shop, a grocer's, and Mary Mancini looked in there to ask, 'Any post for us?'

'There is something . . . Just a minute, there's a parcel somewhere—Luigi! Where's that parcel for Signora Mancini?'

'Back of the slicer and there's a letter as well.'

The parcel and letter were run to earth but not before the grocer's wife had taken in the presence of the Marshal whom she recognized, though she didn't know him to speak to.

'We've insured ourselves, you know,' she said, speaking to him now.

'Insured . . . ?'

'The façade. Of course, we're the ones most at risk what with people in and out of the shop all day. I said to Signora Mancini, we'll be the ones to get sued, and they can't start work on it before June—I said to them, there's lumps of cement the size of a Parmesan cheese coming down. You get hit by one of those and that's it. But we're covered, my husband'll tell you about the policy—Luigi!'

'No, no, you don't need to call Luigi.' It was Mary Mancini who rescued the Marshal, breaking off from examining her parcel. 'The Marshal's come to talk to me about that friend of mine they buried this morning.'

'Oh . . . Not the one who—'

'That's right. But he's in a hurry now so we'll be going up.'

It wasn't that easy. The Marshal, accustomed to this sort of thing, didn't think for a minute that it would be. There was some discussion about the parcel which hadn't had to be signed for but of course if it had been necessary to sign for it they would have signed for it, if that was all right with the signora, only these days you never know and you don't want to go signing things that people wouldn't have wanted to sign if they'd known—of course, in this case it hadn't had to be signed for, at least she didn't think it had, but it was Luigi who took the post this morning because she was serving, but she was pretty sure he'd said he hadn't needed to—Luigi!

'Sorry,' Mary Mancini said when at last they got out, 'but everybody likes a bit of attention and I'm so often out when the post comes—besides, it's an old habit and they'd be offended if I told the postman to ring. He wouldn't get in anyway with this wretched door.'

She rang the bell beside the gigantic oak doors and stood back to look up. After a moment a long-haired girl opened a window two floors up, looked down at them and vanished.

'Hers is the only key that will work at the moment. Won't be a minute . . .'

The girl reappeared above them and launched a huge iron key which Mary caught deftly.

'Practice, you know.'

The door didn't open easily even then and when it did the Marshal had to help her heave it inwards until it began to swing under its own weight. Finding himself in almost complete darkness, the Marshal took off his glasses.

It must have been a fairly elegant house once. The staircase was broad and the high ceiling of the ground-floor area was supported by stone pillars. But there were bicycles and mopeds piled everywhere, the walls were pitted, and the usual background smell of mediæval drains was heavily overlain with a sweet and cloying scent like vanilla.

'Do be careful,' Mary warned him, 'we can't get the condominium to splurge on anything bigger than a five watt light-bulb—the smell comes from the ground floor back, by the way. They make cakes for the bars. It's a bit sickly but I suppose we hardly notice it after twenty years. Come in.'

'Thank you. It's nice and warm in here.' It was very untidy too but in a cheerful way that told of a lot of family activity and too little time to tidy it all up.

'Excuse the mess. It only seems warm because you're so cold. It's a difficult house to heat. We'll stay in the kitchen where it's warmest and I'll make us a hot drink. Take your coat off.'

The kitchen had a window giving on to the garden of the convent in the next street. The top of a huge evergreen tree was swaying frantically in the wind but the sun coming through the glass made the room as warm as toast.

'Caffellatte all right?'

'That would be nice.' He watched her making it, feeling completely at ease as though he'd known her for years. Perhaps that was because she was so at ease with herself. She was as tall as the Marshal, and very relaxed and sure in her movements. Her light brown hair was going grey and she had very deep blue eyes. She didn't wear any make-up. She looked nice like that, the Marshal thought. A nice woman in every way.

'Thank you.'

'Sugar's on the table.' She sat down opposite him, warming her hands around her cup. 'How did you get on with Father Jameson?'

'I liked him.'

'He's a dear. Was he able to help you?'

'A little. Well, a lot. Galli, the journalist, you know him?' She nodded. 'He was the one who said something must have happened between Forbes and his wife at Christmas, and that's when she went to see Father Jameson—or happened to see him. But Father Jameson pointed out that things tend to come to a head at Christmas and I think he's right about that.'

'Did she tell him what it was?'

'No, no . . . She said she was ashamed.'

'Ashamed? I can't imagine Celia—Unless she was ashamed of something Julian had done. She was protective and I suppose there was her pride involved too.'

'Yes . . .' However comfortable he felt with her it wasn't an easy question to ask. Even so, he'd no choice but to ask it. 'He gave me to understand . . .' He looked into the deep blue eyes for help. 'He gave me to understand that he . . .'

Help came. 'Made an attempt on my virtue, as they say? He actually told you that?'

'Well . . . What he told me was that he succeeded.'

'*What?* You didn't believe him?'

'I didn't believe him or disbelieve him, not knowing either of you. Galli told me it was rubbish.'

'Yes. But it's very odd as well, isn't it? I mean—you don't think Celia killed herself, do you?'

'No, no . . .'

'Then you must have some suspicions about him. I have, I can promise you, and I don't imagine you'd be here if you hadn't, so why should he make things look even worse for himself than they are?'

'I don't know. And now that I've met you I can't think how he could have taken it into his head even to try—'

He stopped, dismayed at what must, after all, have sounded like an insult, though it wasn't. 'I don't mean—'

'I know exactly what you mean.' She smiled at him. 'I'm not offended. I'll take it as a sort of compliment. Thank you. Poor Celia. No, you haven't understood what he was after. It wasn't sex. He never struck me as being highly sexed. It was his own ego he was interested in, not our bodies.'

'Our?'

'Oh yes. He didn't tell you all of it, then?'

'You were the only one he named but he did say there were others.'

Mary gave a grim smile. 'Well, there weren't, of course,

any more than there was me, if you understand me. Oh yes, he tried it on with every single one of Celia's friends. Systematically, one after the other, and one after the other we turned him down.'

'It was no secret, then?'

'Certainly not. I gave him a good talking-to, sent him away with a flea in his ear. But I was sure he'd try else-where, so I checked. There were five I knew about. He was impotent with Celia and had been for some time and this was his way of punishing her and trying to prove we loved him as much as her, that he was as brilliant and important as her. Well, we didn't and he wasn't. It's a funny thing, isn't it? The world's full of adoring wives, proud of their husbands' success, but it doesn't seem to work the other way round.'

'Perhaps if he'd had some success himself . . .'

'The adoring wives don't. They just bask.'

'They were married, were they? The name on her passport . . .'

'Oh, yes, she went on using Carter, partly because of Jenny, partly because she was known as a writer, but she did marry him. I often think she regretted it, though she never said so. They'd lived together up till then and I've a feeling things had already gone wrong and she was trying to right them, you know how people do—like those women who get pregnant to save their marriage. Anyway, it didn't work and his trying to take her closest friends to bed was one of his ways of taking, or trying to take, what was hers. Another charming little trick of his was to be present when-ever any journalist came to interview her, especially here in Florence. In London she could arrange things better. The house there is big and anyway there was always the pub and so on. But here, in that little barn, she'd have had to throw him out physically unless he discreetly dis-appeared of his own accord, and of course he never did.'

'He'd sit in and listen?'

'Listen? Not on your life! The journalist—in one case it was me doing an interview for an English colour supplement—would ask Celia some question and, before she could open her mouth, he'd answer it, and at length, talking about her work as though she weren't there, or as though . . .'

'As though she were dead?'

'Do you know, I think I was going to say that, though it hadn't crossed my mind. He'll be her literary executor, won't he? He'll take her royalties, re-edit her books and put his name on them . . . He'll probably even write a book about her, make himself an entire career on her poor dead bones—and he's plausible enough, you know, to anyone who doesn't really know him! Didn't you find that?'

'Well, my first sight of him he was lying dead drunk next door to his wife's body, so . . . Does he always drink a lot?'

Mary sipped her coffee and frowned, thinking. 'Mm. No. Not if you mean actually getting drunk. Usually he just drank what the rest of us drink, but it's funny . . . I'm trying to think . . . those few times I've seen him drunk and he's passed out—of course I've no way of knowing whether he'd been drinking elsewhere so I can't swear to it, but I'm almost certain that he hadn't drunk much more than anyone else.'

'You think perhaps he took something, drugs of some sort?'

'No. I know what it was. He was frightened. I'm sure of it. It was when he was frightened. One time was after I'd had that episode with him. We were at Galli's house to supper and, if you'll believe me, he tried it on again, touching me and asking me to let him come and see me. Celia was in the room. I told him then that I intended going to see Celia and telling her and that I knew about the others. He was terrified. Dinner started, and before we got to the main course he excused himself and went to the bathroom. He never came back, and Celia eventually found him out cold on their hosts' bed. Now, you see, he couldn't have drunk that much—What is it?'

The Marshal turned. The young girl who had thrown down the key was at the kitchen door. She said something to her mother which the Marshal didn't understand.

'Speak Italian, please,' her mother reminded her gently, indicating the Marshal.

'I'm sorry.' The girl offered him her hand. 'I'm Katy. Have you come about Jenny's mother?'

'They're friends,' Mary explained, 'or at least they're at university together. Katy brought her home, you know. That's what the delay was—Katy had an exam. We didn't think Jenny should travel alone. I just wish I could have persuaded her to stay here.'

'You *should* have done, Mum. I don't think she should stay with that crazy old Sissi. She'll be miserable!'

'I couldn't force her, now could I—How many sweaters have you got on, you comic?'

'Five!' The girl laughed at herself, pulling the largest of them down over her wool clad knees, 'And leg lag! It's freezing in my room.'

Her mother reached up and put an arm round her. 'Oh, come and sit here with us. You can tell the Marshal about Jenny.'

'There's not much to tell about Jenny! Mum, you didn't answer my original question, as per usual.'

'I've forgotten what it was . . .'

'As per usual! Shall I put the water on for pasta?'

'Go on then.' Mary glanced at her watch. 'The boss'll be home in ten minutes. Not my husband,' she explained to the Marshal, 'he doesn't come home for lunch. The boss is my youngest—we have a seventeen-year-old son as well—Lizzy's only six.'

'She's Mum's mistake!' Katy heaved the big pan on to the cooker and then collapsed in giggles.

'You shut up and sit down. It happens in the best of families.'

Katy sat down with them, her numerous sleeves pulled down over her cold hands.

'Mum, what are we going to do about Jenny? Shall I try and make her come out with us tonight so it'll be too late to get back and she'll have to stay over?'

Mary looked doubtful. 'I'd wait till tomorrow. It doesn't seem right on the same day as the funeral. What do you think?'

It was the Marshal's opinion she was asking and it pleased him. 'I'd say tomorrow. Are you good friends?'

'Oh, you know . . . We're at the same university and our parents are friends so we have to be.'

'You don't like her?'

'It's not that. I feel sorry for her, I suppose. She's cleverer than me, at least I think she is, but she takes a week to write an essay when it takes me a few hours. And she never goes out, just sits thumping away at the piano.'

'Not everybody wants to be a social butterfly like you,' Mary pointed out.

'Social butterfly! Mum, you're so old-fashioned—anyway, I don't see why playing the piano should stop her going out, or having a boyfriend, but she never has anybody. They take her out once because she's so nice-looking but she never speaks. Honestly, I'm not kidding, she sits there like a stick for hours, answering Yes or No if you ask her anything.'

'She doesn't confide in you, then?' The Marshal asked, his last hope fading, 'She didn't tell you about some sort of upset with her mother over Christmas?'

'No . . . we didn't see them at Christmas, though, did we, Mum?'

'They were meant to have Christmas dinner here,' Mary explained, 'but they cried off at the last minute.'

'And when you went back after the holiday? You didn't notice any difference in her?' The Marshal looked from Katy to Mary, 'If her mother was in such a state . . .'

'She did get thinner,' Katy said, thinking. 'Not that she was ever fat but she got really, really thin after Christmas. She still is. You noticed, didn't you, Mum?'

'You're thinking of drugs, aren't you?' Mary asked the Marshal.

'Oh, *Mum*!'

'Katy, you can't always tell, just like that.'

'*You* can't always tell, my generation can. Everybody knows exactly what everybody else is on!'

'You mean you're all on something? Katy, you're not—'

'Oh, *Mum*! For goodness' sake! Jenny wasn't on anything except perhaps a diet. Anyway, she didn't tell me anything if there was anything to tell. Even so, I bet she was pissed off with Julian and I don't blame her. I can't stick him. Every time I see him he asks what I'm studying and then gives me a lecture on it.'

'He's only trying to help, I suppose,' Mary said.

'To show off, more like. I don't want him helping me. Jenny has to put up with it but I don't. She said she wouldn't have got through her A levels without him but how does she know she wouldn't? Wait a minute . . .'

'You've remembered something about Christmas?' The Marshal looked at her hopefully.

'Sort of—I mean, it was before Christmas. I wanted to book our tickets to come home and you have to do that really early at Christmastime to get a seat. We'd been at a lecture and everybody was leaving. She was packing her notebooks and I pushed along to where she was sitting.

'"Listen, my money's come. I could go and book our tickets this afternoon. Are you coming with me?"

'She just shook her head and carried on putting her stuff away.

'"You'll have to buck up, you know, or there'll be no seats."

'She still didn't answer. "If you haven't got the money we can use mine for a deposit on both and then when—"

'"I can't!"

'"For God's sake, Jenny, what's the difference—"

'"I can't. I'm not going."

'"Well, where are you going to go? Not that you have to tell me your business, but I can't see you going on holiday by yourself or spending Christmas alone in that great rambling house in London."

'She didn't tell me, of course. She burst into tears—she does that sometimes if you try and make her talk. It's useless. Anyway, I didn't think of all that right away, because in the end she did come, so goodness knows what was up with her that day.'

The Marshal sat a moment looking out at the tormented treetop outside the window. He was thoroughly warm himself now but the angry whine of the wind sent a little shiver through him at the thought of the bitter cold out there. Or at the thought . . .

'You don't think—' it was Mary who put his half idea into words—'that he didn't want the child there because he . . . you know . . . didn't want a witness. But she came anyway and he had to put off . . .'

'The furniture . . .' the Marshal said, as though he hadn't heard a word. 'He changed the furniture without his wife's knowledge, though presumably with her money. There was something very wrong about that. He didn't like my knowing. And he said it was a Christmas present.'

'You're right!' Mary said. 'There was a divan there that opened into a double bed. That's where Jenny slept up until then. That Christmas she had to stay at Sissi's like she's doing now. He didn't want her there, then. I'm right. It wasn't Celia, I'll never believe that. She adored Jenny, she was the light of her life. He didn't want her and he got rid of the only place she could sleep. No wonder she cried. If only she'd told you, Katy, then you could have brought her here.'

'But she didn't tell me. She never tells anybody anything. She just sits there like she was modelling for a Botticelli painting and if you try and shake her out of it she cries.'

The Marshal was dismayed. He would have to talk to the girl, but he didn't fancy his chances of success with a Botticelli painting that wept real tears. Well, it had to be faced, though he'd have preferred to spend the rest of his day in that cosy kitchen. Mary accompanied him downstairs since she had to meet the school bus at the door.

'You must have your hands full with three children and working as a journalist as well.'

'Oh, I gave up the full-time stuff when Lizzy was born. I write for the monthlies, so I'm not fraught with deadlines. You know, we almost nicknamed our little Elizabeth Sissi instead of Lizzy but she might have thought it cruel. She's a dear old thing, potty or not.'

'Cruel? Wouldn't she be flattered?'

'Ah, you don't know the background. Sissi's parents gave her that name after the Austrian Empress who was so famous for her beauty. Our poor Sissi was as ugly as sin even as a tiny child. I've seen photos of her. She shows them to you and makes out it's a fine joke her parents made at her expense. But you can't tell me she didn't suffer because of it. Our bossy little Lizzy's a beauty. It might look like rubbing it in—Here she comes!'

A yellow minibus with a seething burden of small children inside was coming towards them. Before it came to a stop Mary looked hard at the Marshal. 'Don't answer, of course, if I shouldn't ask, but do you think he might have killed her?'

'I've no evidence for it.' His eyes were invisible behind dark glasses. His voice was devoid of expression.

She understood him.

'Chopin!' Sissi managed to hiss a great deal of contempt into the word, making no further comment necessary. Nevertheless, she gave the Marshal a sharp prod with her finger and added, 'Bach!' Settling the matter. She then stumped along in front of the Marshal and Fara, so that they only got the briefest glimpse of the girl in a room to their left. Her back was to the door as she played, a back rigid as a statue's, with heavy coils of blonde hair hanging behind to her waist.

'Relax those fingers!' roared Sissi over her shoulder. She hustled them into the bookfilled study where she had first fallen asleep, smiling at the Marshal. The piano music was still audible. Sometimes it faltered, then began again with more determination.

'Sit down,' ordered Sissi. 'I might as well warn you, she doesn't talk much, might not talk at all to you, so don't be surprised.'

They sat down in comfortable armchairs. Outside the arched window they could see the rows of cypresses, their tops thrashing frantically. It was very warm in the little room which was heated by a stove in one corner. A small glazed dish holding an apple stood on the flat surface of the stove. Sissi showed her teeth at the Marshal when she saw his puzzled glance.

'My apple. Put it there in the morning and the heat bakes it slowly. Eat it at five. Very good.'

'I'm sure it is.' It certainly gave a sweet and welcoming smell to the warm room. Young Fara was gazing about him at the heavy foreign-looking furniture and the hundreds of pictures and books. The Marshal remembered the package he was carrying and consigned it to Sissi.

'Ah! Enjoyed it?'

'Yes . . . yes, thank you for lending it to me.'

'A prompt returner of books. Knew you would be or I wouldn't have lent it. I'll send the girl. Remember she doesn't speak much. Families!' A word that came spitting through the chipmunk teeth with a venom that left Chopin far behind. 'She'll be better off without.'

The Marshal frowned. 'From what I understand, her mother was very much attached to her.'

'Oh yes. Also successful, very clever. My mother was beautiful. Got out. Best thing. Listen!'

They listened. She was playing something different now. The Marshal thought it sounded very nice, and he was impressed.

'You see. Plays badly, very badly but she needn't. It's all a question of nerves.'

'Well, I'm no judge . . .'

'Phuh! I'll get her.'

When she'd gone, Fara, with a pink-faced glance at the Marshal, got out a notebook and pen. The Marshal's face remained expressionless but there was a lot going on behind his blank eyes.

The fact that Fara was sitting there with the Marshal, notebook at the ready, was largely thanks to Mary Mancini. In the car on the way up here, Fara had, after a lot of stuttering, asked permission to follow the case more closely.

'I feel I can learn a lot. That is, if you . . .'

And the Marshal, embarrassed, remembered Mary Mancini's saying he looked intelligent . . .

And he obviously worships you.

While that in itself was nonsense, it was true that he'd neglected the lad, embroiled as he was in his own troubles.

If he was happy sitting there taking notes, well, it was harmless enough and might even turn out useful.

He had only just registered the fact that the piano music had stopped, when the door opened quietly and the girl was standing there. The diminutive Sissi, all but invisible behind her, must have given her a push.

'Go on!' Before shutting the door she added with some emphasis, 'I'll be right here!' Though who among them she thought might require rescuing was unclear.

Both men had stood up when the door opened, and now they hovered uncertainly, expecting the girl to tell them to sit down again or at least be seated herself, but she didn't move. She remained very still, her hands folded in front of her, looking at them. She seemed utterly composed but there was a rigidity in her stance that suggested otherwise. There was no avoiding the Botticelli image, despite her wearing faded jeans and a worn black sweater. It wasn't just the long heavy hair, more something to do with her stillness, watchful and self-contained.

It was the Marshal who had to suggest they sat down. Even seated, she didn't lean back in the big chair but remained upright, her back as rigid as ever, her brown eyes fixed on his. She folded her long white hands quietly in her lap. The Marshal, prepared for her silence, was startled when she was the first to speak.

'I don't want to talk about her.'

'Your mother? Of course, so soon after the funeral . . . I'm sorry we had to do this, but it is necessary.'

She received this in silence, no longer looking directly at him but at some point in space to one side of him. He tightened his grip on the hat parked on his knee and with a little cough insisted.

'You're very young and you've had a bad shock, but you're old enough to realize, I think, that we're obliged, in the circumstances, to make inquiries . . .'

Nothing. When it came down to it she didn't look old enough. She had the air of a child, obedient but unresponsive, so unresponsive that it crossed his mind that perhaps she wasn't normal. He'd seen mad people retreat into their own heads like that—yet she was at university and neither Mary Mancini nor her daughter, sane, sensible people, had suggested there might be something wrong with her. He sighed inwardly. His only experience of a wall of silence so impenetrable was with dull-witted and patently guilty criminals. That brute Saverino had been one of them. Hadn't opened his mouth until the trial. It had been the pathetic little Pecchioli who'd told all.

With less tough characters a few days in the cells often did the trick, but he could hardly lock up this fair and delicate creature. He tried another tack.

'What I'd really like to talk about is you.'

'Me? Why should you be interested in me?'

It wasn't much but it was better than silence. 'I'm sure a lot of people are interested in you, in how you're feeling, what you intend to do.'

She shrugged her shoulders.

'You'll continue at university?'

A shrug, this time evidently meaning, 'I suppose so.'

'You'll be independent now, economically and . . . in every way. You might feel there's something else you'd prefer to do.'

'I'll never do anything!' She almost shouted it at him and her face changed colour. She was surely about to cry. The Marshal gave an unhappy glance at the door, knowing that Sissi would be listening in. This was going as badly as his visit to Forbes, when, trying to work his way around dangerous areas, he had set off a mine with an innocent remark about the furniture. Well, so be it.

'I'm sure that's not true. You have every advantage.

You're obviously a bright girl, studying at university—Italian, isn't it?'

A nod.

'Which you already speak well. You're very pretty and you'll have more than enough money for your needs. Most girls would envy you.'

Her only response was a downward twist at one corner of her mouth whose meaning was not lost on the Marshal. Though often accused of not following what people were saying, he was always aware of what they were thinking. That disdainful little smirk said that he didn't know what he was talking about.

'Have you given any thought at all to a career?'

'I'll have to teach, I suppose.'

'But you don't want to, judging by the way you say it.'

He wondered how she imagined she'd be able to teach without the aid of the spoken word. He looked at her hands lying one over the other, smooth and flawless with short, very white nails. Not a tremor. They lay as still as dead birds. He had a distressing feeling that he wasn't just dealing with shyness or even a chronic lack of confidence, that the apparently perfect creature was somehow irreparably damaged. Her mother, who had loved her, had grieved for her as a lost child. When he looked up at her face again she stared back at him accusingly.

'You're not interested in me, you're here because of my mother and how she died.'

'Do you know how she died—I mean, do you know any more than we do?'

'How should I know? I wasn't even here.'

'You might know from Forbes.'

Silence. A silence that might have lasted indefinitely if the Marshal, as much to break it as anything, asked, 'You aren't disturbed by my carabiniere taking notes? He can leave if you prefer it.' But she only shrugged. Fara looked at the Marshal for guidance but he, too, shrugged. What was the point? He might as well stay. The poor lad hadn't written a word, anyway. What was there to write?

'Did you quarrel with your mother, Signorina? At Christmas, or a little before?'

'No.'

'But she was very distressed at that time about you. Had you been in some trouble in England?'

'No.'

'You can't think of any reason why she should have been so distressed about you?'

'She was disappointed in me, I suppose. I'm not as bright as she expected.'

'And was Julian Forbes disappointed in you, too?'
Silence.

'He used to help you with your school work, your friend Katy told me. Did he get bored with you because you were not as bright as he expected, either?'

That, at least, touched a spot. She stared at him in hatred and her face flushed deep red.

'He didn't want you here any more, did he?'

'It was her, she was the one who wrote—'

'No, no . . . I can promise you that she was deeply grieved about it. If you fought with your mother and accused her—'

'She even sold my bed!'

'No. He did. He was very jealous, my dear, and he wanted himself at the centre of everything. You shouldn't have blamed your mother. I realize that it's an unhappy thought for you now that it's too late to make up your quarrel, but it's important for you, and will be throughout your life, to know that your mother loved you very deeply. And you did come for Christmas in the end, didn't you?'

She nodded, again with that downward twist of her mouth.

'Your mother must have been the one who told you to come.'

She nodded miserably.

'I suppose it wasn't a very happy visit after what had happened. It may be that, in the end, your mother decided to leave her husband because of his rejection of you. Doesn't that say that she cared a lot about you?'

She was staring past him in silence again. The Marshal persisted a little while longer, chiefly in the hope of persuading her to go and stay with the Mancini family, but he elicited no further replies. Her tension disturbed him deeply. He had in a fairly long career dealt with many bereaved people. Some were hysterical, some unbelieving, some collapsed from the shock and others almost attacked him physically as the bearer of bad tidings. Never had he encountered this paralysing tension. It was affecting him so badly that he had to bring the interview to a close. It was a relief to get to his feet and make for the door with Fara behind him. The girl didn't move from her chair. Sissi opened up as he was reaching out his hand for the doorknob.

'I could hardly hear half of it,' she complained, 'I'm always having to tell that girl to speak up—when she *does* speak—but I didn't think you'd have been a mumbler.'

As they returned to their car by the lemon pots in their furiously snapping polythene shrouds, they glimpsed the worried face of the Signora Torrini gazing down at them from an upper floor window. There was no sign of life in the barn, no face behind the lattice-work.

'We're not going in to see him, then?' Fara ventured to ask.

'He's not there,' the Marshal said, 'there's no fire lit and it's well below freezing point.'

Fara looked up. It was true that no curl of smoke was coming from the chimney. The sky above, seared by the icy wind, burned a deep, pure blue such as was never seen in summer.

'I wish I lived in this place,' Fara said, gazing out at the villa as he turned the ignition.

'The people who do,' observed the Marshal, 'don't seem to be enjoying it much.'

The Marshal lay in bed rolling the day's images through his mind and enjoying the sound of Teresa chattering to him as she pottered in and out tidying away their day.

'The fishmonger says they'll never in this world dare arrest the hunchback—he always calls him that, never uses his name, but of course he's a communist, so . . . but that retired professor was in, I forget his name but you met him once at the opening of that exhibition so you know who I mean, he buys a lot of fish, doesn't care for meat, and *he* said that that written defence he'd submitted to the magistrates was a typical Mafia document, the language used, the reasoning, everything—do *you* think he'll ever be arrested? Salva? Salva!'

'What? I don't know . . .' He plugged himself into the conversation and ran it back a bit. 'You didn't make any comment, I hope?'

'Of course not. I must say it's nice to have the boys back.'

It was. They'd burst in, sunburnt, grubby and noisier than ever. Dropping rucksacks, polythene bags and anoraks in a trail through the flat, shouting each other down with stories, complaints, jokes and confessions, it had been like having the *tramontana* rip straight through the house. Now all was peace as they slept the sleep of the exhausted and contented.

There had been one brief interlude of discontent, however, only shortly after their arrival. Teresa brought it up now as she slid into bed.

'Why didn't you let them go, by the way?'

'What?'

'Why didn't you let them go for the end-of-trip pizza with all the others tonight? The teachers were going, they'd have been all right.'

'They've just had a week's holiday.'

'Well, it was only to round it off. It was a nice idea.'

'They have too much. They're spoilt.'

'Even so, it's not like you. You usually like them to enjoy themselves.'

She received no further enlightenment on the subject and so left it at that, to observe after a few minutes' silence, 'Have you noticed how quiet it is?'

'Mm?'

'I was thinking it was because the boys had gone to bed but it's not. The wind's dropped.'

It was true. Not a sound disturbed them from outside their shutters.

'Thank goodness for that.'

'Thank goodness is right,' Teresa said, turning over and settling down. 'It was so tiring battling against it. It should be lovely tomorrow if it doesn't cloud over again right away.'

'It won't.' He lay awake after her, turning over some doubts in his mind. He wondered whether it had been the right thing to let Fara go over later to take a look in at Il Caffè in case Forbes turned up and ... well, and what? He hadn't wanted to discourage the lad and it was true that he'd been inconspicuous and that Forbes would never recognize him out of uniform ... well, it couldn't do any harm ...

The other thing he had doubts about was much less clearly defined. He had been sure all along that Forbes had murdered his wife and now he was sure why. She must have decided to leave him. If she had, he'd have been jobless, homeless, penniless and by all accounts friendless. Another golden goose like Celia Carter wouldn't be easy to come by. Even so, he wasn't convinced. He felt he was seeing all the component parts of the picture but not seeing the meaning that held it all together. When, later, he did see it, he was forced to admit to himself that he'd been trying to avoid it, that he preferred on this windless, peaceful night, to push his doubts to one side and concentrate on getting a good night's sleep.

After all, he reasoned, as he slid deeper into the warmth of the big bed, it didn't much matter what he knew or didn't know since he had no hope of ever proving anything. Before he quite dropped off he opened his eyes to check that the alarm on his bedside cabinet was set. It was. The luminous hands said a quarter to midnight. He closed his eyes.

Out in the still winter night, the temperature climbed steadily. Needles of gold light glittered in the dark waters of the Arno beneath the Ponte Vecchio where the silence of the deserted city was being rudely broken by Julian Forbes, drunk and bloodied, resisting arrest by the police.

CHAPTER 9

'How long did he stay at Il Caffè?' The Marshal sat down at his desk as he asked the question. The pink-faced Fara had barely let him get into the office, so full was he of his story.

'Not so long, not much more than an hour. I got there well before him. He arrived at half past ten.' He consulted his notebook, 'Ten twenty-seven.'

'And was this girl with him or did he pick her up there?'

'She came in with him. He was all over her. He insisted on trailing round the whole room to speak to everyone he knew and introduce her. He was feeling her the whole time, and she looked a bit uncomfortable, but she didn't stop him.'

'And where were you, that he didn't spot you going around like that?'

'Up on the balcony. It's tiny, just four tables lined up, but there are potted palms and stuff and very low lights, romantic. The only thing was they're all couples up there, so I felt a bit stupid, anyway . . . When he'd buttonholed everybody he could think of they sat down near Galli who was there with a tall blonde woman.'

'His wife.'

'I suppose it would have been, he didn't talk to her much. He didn't talk to Forbes much either and you could tell he didn't want him there, kept turning his back and getting deep into conversation with another journalist—I don't know his name but I've seen him around. I saw him going into court the other day when I was waiting for you. Forbes kept trying to butt in, but Galli must have said something pretty sharp, so in the end he gave up and started slopping all over this girl he was with. Then he managed to persuade another girl who was leaving to sit down and have a drink with them. After that, he had an arm round each girl and was talking nineteen to the dozen. I couldn't hear what he was saying because there's always music playing. The second girl was the first to leave. I don't think Forbes wanted to move but his girlfriend persuaded him.'

'Was he drunk?'

'I suppose . . . I don't know. He looked—feverish. You know? Excited. I suppose he might have drunk a lot of wine at dinner before going there, but he only had two drinks— marc de champagne both times, I heard the waiter. I don't think anybody'd be likely to get drunk in that place because there's nothing costs less than eight thousand lire . . .'

He tailed off, embarrassed. The Marshal fished some money out of his pocket. Fara's face got redder.

'I didn't mean . . .'

'Take it. You can't afford that, son. I should have thought on. You didn't keep the receipt?'

'Of course, but I threw it away when I got in. I wasn't intending . . .'

'Well, another time keep it. So, you don't think he was drunk?'

'Not really. Like I said, he was excited. He started raising his voice a bit, and I think that's why the girl wanted to leave.'

'He was raising his voice at her?'

'Oh no. I think at Galli. I think Galli must have offended him, though I couldn't hear. Then he turned his back. Forbes shouted then. I heard him say "a bunch of hacks", which meant the journalists, I suppose, then he pointed to himself, prodding his chest, no doubt telling them he was something a cut above. Luckily the girl managed to get him out and I rushed downstairs to follow them. I didn't know, of course, about the bike.'

The bike was one of those enormous efforts—Fara apologized for not being well-informed enough to distinguish the make—with engines as big as a car's, and bristling all over with accessories.

'He must have bought it that day. It glittered with newness.'

When he saw the two of them mount the monster motorbike, Fara had intended to give the thing up and cross back to the Pitti.

'Only they went the wrong way, roaring along the Via Guicciardini towards the Ponte Vecchio. I knew they wouldn't get far before they were stopped, going back up a one-way street like that. So I strolled along, listening. The streets were very quiet because, at that time everything's shut round here except Il Caffè.'

'And were they stopped?'

'Of course they were. I didn't see the very start of the business, but once I heard the commotion I started running. Evidently he'd managed to get between the bollards that keep the traffic off the bridge. I heard a whistle blow, a bit of a roar and then a crash. When I arrived on the scene a little group of spectators had appeared out of nowhere, so I mixed in with them and watched.'

'What was the crash? Had he come off the motorbike?'

'From what I could gather he must have got on the bridge and two municipal police—a man and a woman—had waved him down. I suppose they whistled when he didn't stop, and when I arrived they were yelling at him that he could easily have killed them. As it was he'd run into the bollards at the other end. The girl hadn't a scratch on her, but Forbes's face was bleeding and one of his hands, too. He was hysterical, screaming at the police that it was their fault and they would pay for it. They asked him for documents but he refused to show any, saying the British ambassador was a personal friend of his and that he would see to it that they lost their jobs. He went on like that for a bit while they were waiting for a patrol car to come and pick him up.'

'And you still don't think he was drunk?' The Marshal didn't want to discourage the lad who, after all, had done a good job, but he couldn't have much experience of the different ways drunkenness can take people.

But Fara, despite his timidity, insisted. 'I know he hit the bollard but he was going too fast, and it was a big bike, I don't think he knew how to control it. He was hysterical—'

'He was also,' interrupted the Marshal gently, 'on the Ponte Vecchio on a motorbike, having got there by going along a one-way street the wrong way.'

'I know, but . . . I mean, everybody does that sometimes. The streets were empty—I don't mean I do it—'

'I didn't think you did,' the Marshal said. 'I take your point. In that case what do you think he was so hysterical about?'

When the boy hesitated he said, 'Come on. You were there and you have your own idea about this, don't you? Let's hear it.'

'I think . . . I think he was hysterical because he was scared.'

'Of being stopped by the Municipal Police?'

'Well, he perhaps had no documents—and who knows if the motorbike was his? We never saw it up at the villa and, anyway, it was brand new, only—we've got his passport and he can't leave, so maybe it's getting to him. Showing off that girl in Il Caffè like he was doing, it's not normal just after the funeral. I think he's doing it on purpose because he's frightened. He must know you suspect him and he's trying to pretend he doesn't care, but he's so hysterical it comes out all wrong . . .'

Fara tailed off because he could see the Marshal wasn't really listening. 'Shall I go and type my report?'

'No, no . . .' The Prosecutor had said that time on the phone, '*You'll probably frighten him to death.*' And then Mary Mancini had said that when Forbes was frightened, a couple of drinks . . . Even so, it wasn't true. It might well be true that Forbes was frightened, but why now? When they had let him bury his wife he ought to have been less frightened. The autopsy hadn't worried him but, apparently, the funeral had sent him into hysterics.

'I'm probably talking rubbish. I just thought—'

'No, no . . . You're not talking rubbish at all. It's quite possible that he does feel threatened, but not by me. Not by me. I wonder . . .'

He had been going to say that another chat to Forbes might be in order, when a commotion in the waiting-room saved him the trouble.

'It's him!' Fara got to his feet. 'He'd better not see me, had he? I mean . . .'

'Don't worry about it. Just go to the duty room.'

Lorenzini knocked and looked in with his eyebrows raised in question. 'Forbes . . .'

'Let him in.' There was hardly the time or the need to say it since Forbes was already pushing past Lorenzini, his bearded chin stabbing the air arrogantly, but his eyes not quite meeting those of the Marshal who gazed at him blandly.

Lorenzini nodded towards the girl Forbes was towing behind him. 'I suggested the young lady stay in the waiting-room . . .'

'She's with me!' The girl was holding three Gucci carrier bags. At a look from the Marshal she seemed only too glad to scuttle out behind Lorenzini, the look on her face suggesting that there was more to this than she had been told.

'Take a seat,' offered the Marshal mildly.

'I'm not here to sit and chat, I'm here for my passport.

I have business to transact in England, lawyers to see. The British consul—'

'Sit down. Or be shown out.'

He sat. He was shaking visibly. A bruise was developing round a cut on his temple.

'That girl,' the Marshal said, 'looks very young.'

'She's over eighteen, if that's what you mean. She's an American student studying history of art. I'm giving her a few pointers.'

'Really.'

'Yes, really. These girls arrive here with no background knowledge at all. They can't be expected to find their way about in the maze of Florentine history.'

'She seems to have found her way to Gucci.'

Forbes tried to sit back in the leather chair and cross one leg over the other. He was so tense he almost found it impossible.

'I took her there, too, if it interests you. I can afford it—though I fail to see what my sex life has to do with you.'

'I didn't know that was what we were talking about. I beg your pardon.'

'Look, I'm here because I need my passport!'

'I'm afraid I don't have it. It's in the office of the Public Prosecutor who will return it to you in due course.'

'Now listen here, I intend to go straight to the British Consulate when I leave this office, and you're going to find—'

'Excuse me.' The Marshal picked up his phone which had rung twice. 'Put him on. Guarnaccia.' The Marshal listened in silence for some time, frowning, his gaze fixed on Forbes's shaking knee. Then he said, 'Can I ask you to hold the line a moment?'

He rang for Lorenzini, who must have been keeping an eye on the girl in the waiting-room because his head came round the door immediately.

'Marshal.'

'Show Mr Forbes into the waiting-room, will you, until I've finished with this call?'

'You can't keep me waiting. I'm getting on to the ambassador. I—'

But Lorenzini was a big man, and the Marshal had already picked up the phone and turned away.

'Captain? I'm sorry. He was here in the room with me.'

'Really? Did you pick him up?'

'No, no . . . it seems to be some sort of social call. He's asking for his passport, but since he can't be stupid enough to think I've got it, or that I'd give it to him if I had, I imagine he was here to show me the girl he's picked up.'

'Girl? Whatever for? Hardly puts him in a good light.'

'No.'

'So why?'

'I don't know. Last night he got himself arrested and I don't know why he did that either.'

'Arrested? By whom?'

'Municipal Police.' The Marshal gave him a brief account of the episode on the Ponte Vecchio.

'Good Lord.'

'Yes. Well, they must have let him loose first thing, probably couldn't stand any more of him. It didn't boil down to much in terms of charges, I suppose, anyway.'

'And neither will this, I'm afraid. It's indicative that Sotheby's called the consul and got him to call me. They can't afford a scandal. They do business on trust. Besides, he didn't actually steal anything so they've just got a very irate client on their hands. A good client, too, it seems, so they're pretty livid.'

'Even so, if the goods are still there . . .'

'But they shouldn't be. They should be sold, and would have been if it hadn't been for Forbes.'

'Yes, well, I'm not sure I know how these things work . . .'

'It's simple enough; he went in there and started bidding for a batch of antique Persian carpets. He outbid everyone and they were marked down to him, but then he vanished. Never turned up to pay or take them. You can imagine that if that sort of thing happens too often the firm's reputation would hit the dust.'

'But . . . Didn't the auctioneer have any doubts?'

'Apparently he did. But of course he knew Forbes by sight as a member of the British community here, knew Celia Carter's highly respectable reputation and so on— and they'd bought one or two things before, nothing grand. And let's face it, knowing about her death—'

'They were counting on his having inherited.'

'I'm afraid so. The god Mammon plays nasty tricks on his worshippers.'

The Marshal thought, privately, that it rather served them right. Without being able to define quite why, he found their reasoning in some way offensive to the dead woman.

'What do they want us to do?'

'Keep him out of their saleroom but not take any official action that would get the story made public.'

'Hmph. You don't want me to provide a man just for that? I can't manage . . .'

'No, don't worry. I'll send somebody for a day or two in the interest of diplomatic relations. But what do you think all this lunatic behaviour means in terms of your case? You don't think he's preparing the way for an insanity defence, as a precaution?'

'I don't know.' It hadn't even crossed his mind. He wished someone more intelligent would take over this business. 'I think, though, unless he does anything too serious, we should let him carry on. Some sort of explanation might offer.'

'You don't think he really is mad?'

'I think he's weak, and nasty with it, or because of it. I'm not qualified to say whether people like him are mad or not, only . . .'

'Only what?'

'Up there at the villa, there are only two old ladies and a very young girl . . .' He didn't finish the sentence and nothing came over the line for a moment until the Captain mentally finished it for him.

'Yes. I see your point. If I can spare a man to hang around Sotheby's . . .'

'I didn't mean quite—'

'Guarnaccia, you did, you did, and you're right. I think I'll have a word with Fusarri and the three of us should get together. There's some stuff through from England on Forbes, I know—by the way, you've no reason to worry about Fusarri's friendship with the woman at the villa— what was her name?'

'Torrini.'

'Torrini, yes. Well, I did mention it to the Colonel and, as it happens, he knows her. Delightful woman, very beautiful, he said, in her day, a bit daffy now.'

'Yes.'

'Well, she's the last person to try and interfere with the course of justice, as they say. He's all right, you know, Fusarri, even though he's a bit odd.'

'Yes.'

'What will you do with Forbes now, boot him out?'

'Yes.'

'I'll let you get on, then, and be in touch when I've talked to Fusarri.' He hung up.

Only when he'd hung up himself did the Marshal have a vague feeling that perhaps he hadn't been very forthcoming with his answers. But the thought was pushed to the back of his mind by an idea about Forbes's behaviour. Not a clear idea—it had almost been clear while the Captain was talking, but he'd lost it. All he could remember was that it had something to do with his poor little friend Vittorio, but what the devil the connection had been he couldn't for the life of him work out. He tried working back logically through Pecchioli who, when he was being cross-examined, had first brought Vittorio to mind, but it was a dead end and he had to give up.

Still frowning and shaking his head at his own incapacity to think logically, he got up and went to the door. Lorenzini had parked himself outside it, facing the two leather armchairs and the low table covered in magazines that filled the small space between the Marshal's office and the door and so constituted the waiting-room. Forbes had taken up his habitual 'None of this bothers me' position, leaning well back with his leg crossed over, affecting to read the official carabinieri magazine, holding it at a distance and pointing his beard rather than his glance at it. Lorenzini stood back to let the Marshal out.

'Get on to the municipal police,' the Marshal told him quickly. 'They picked him up last night. Get their end of the story—and then warn that young lady off.'

'Of course—you don't think it might be more effective coming from you? I mean . . .'

'She won't know the difference. Just got here. You'll have to speak English to her.' The Marshal beckoned to Forbes without a word. Forbes stood up, said something to the girl and strode, his head a little too high, into the Marshal's office.

'Sit down.' He didn't pretend this time.

'You're getting quite famous,' the Marshal informed him, taking his own seat. 'News of you coming in from everywhere. I hear you've bought yourself a motorbike.'

'Yes. It's something I always fancied doing—and the sort of thing to do while you're young. You probably know by now that my wife was considerably older than me. We lived rather a quiet life.'

It was fortunate that the Marshal's Sicilian blood told. His face betrayed nothing of his reaction to this remark.

'I know you'll pardon my asking—you know how it is, once a policeman, always a policeman, even in ordinary conversation—how did you pay for it? A cheque? Cash? Promissory notes, perhaps?'

'I—I paid a deposit and . . . Promissory notes, why not?'

'Why not, indeed. Of course the law comes down very hard . . . Still, anyone with a regular monthly income can make their calculations accordingly . . .'

Forbes's lack of a monthly income at this point was left drifting on the air. It was a long shot, since Celia Carter might well have provided for this by a banker's order which would still be effective. The silence indicated otherwise.

'Ah well,' the Marshal went on cosily, 'you'll have inherited a goodish bit of money, I dare say.'

'Enough.' Forbes's expression was supremely arrogant but still his eyes never quite met those of the Marshal whose unblinking gaze was fixed on the quivering figure before him.

'Usually takes six months or so to prove a will, though, or does it? I'm no expert. Nobody ever left me anything except their relations and funeral bills.'

'I can imagine.'

'Yes. Well, six months soon passes—and I've heard that the lawyers are usually reasonable about advancing a bit of money, if only to pay for the funeral—Ah! When I think about it, our investigations might have messed things up a bit there. Now that I think about it, the Public Prosecutor will have been in touch with—oh, but there's the young lady, your stepdaughter. No reason why they shouldn't advance money to her. That means she'll pay for the funeral.'

'She did, as a matter of fact. Why not?'

'Yes. Of course, you'll be able to reimburse her when things get sorted out . . .'

'What things?'

The Marshal chose to ignore this. 'Well, what are your plans now?'

'What?'

'I'm sorry. You were kind enough to call on me so I thought . . . I didn't intend to pry into your business. Just a sociable inquiry, you know. I thought you might be thinking of buying a house . . .'

The pale eyes met his for a fleeting instant and veered away. Young Fara wasn't far wrong. They were feverish.

'I have got my eye on something, as it happens, but I'd prefer not to mention it until it's settled, if you don't mind.'

The Marshal, face bland and innocent, opened his hands in total submission. 'You'll think I'm prying again. No, no . . . it was just the carpets that made me think . . . natural association, as you can imagine.'

'I can imagine, yes. Those stuffed frogs from Sotheby's have been talking. Well, it's a lot of fuss about nothing. I'll go round there and collect them when I have time. At the moment, I've rather a lot on my mind, you know that.'

'I do, indeed. Was there anything else?'

'What?' Forbes looked alarmed. It was clear that he had quite forgotten that he was the one to initiate this little meeting. Now he didn't know how to get out of the room.

The Marshal, who found his presence oppressive in the extreme, decided to help him. 'I don't want to delay you for your appointment with the British consul . . .'

Forbes had been trying, during the last part of this conversation to tip his chair back in a careless attitude. When the Marshal suddenly got to his feet and came round the desk towards him he almost fell backwards. The Marshal, it was true, was three times his weight, but it wasn't so much that as his presence, his gravity, that made Forbes dither. Beads of sweat appeared on his temples, though the room was not too warm. Saving himself from falling backwards, he jumped to his feet and was swept towards the door merely by the force of the Marshal's stare.

'Allow me.' The Marshal opened up. 'Your girlfriend seems to have deserted you.' He stopped on the threshold of his office and watched Forbes scuttle in silence across the bit of waiting-room where Lorenzini waited at the door and ceremoniously saluted him out, following the retreating figure with a grimace.

'The girl left,' he said, locking the door.

'So I see. What did she have to say for herself?'

'She was furious. Seems he told her he was coming here to report the theft of a camera. She got wind there was something up, and I told her she was right, there was. She's only eighteen. Beats me what an eighteen-year-old sees in him.'

'He gives them pointers.'

'Eh?'

'That's what he says. You'd have to be no more than eighteen to fall for it, his great knowledge of Florentine art and history and what-have-you.'

'What's that got to do with it? He looks like he couldn't get it up to me.'

'Yes. Well, people are peculiar. It's not our problem. What we need to know is why he brought her here.'

'Just trailing her along?'

'Oh no. No, no. He brought her to show her to me.'

'But why—Well, yes, as you said, we don't know why.'

'Hm.' The Marshal turned back to go into his office. 'That's the trouble, damn it. I do know why, I just can't remember . . .'

He closed the door. Lorenzini stared after him for a moment and then turned to the duty room, shouting, 'Fara!'

'Mortified! I'm just mortified! Nobody ever comes to see me and now all of you are here and I can't even—'

'Eugenia!' Fusarri put an arm round her and almost carried her to the door of the sitting-room to eject her.

'If I could just offer you a cup of tea! If I'd known before one, when Giorgio calls, I'd have told him to organize something with Doney but although I make tea for myself it's a teapot for one and I can't possibly reach the top of the cupboard where the others are—there's an English one— Doulton—and a Japanese one that Giorgio—'

'Eugenia!' He shut the door on her. 'Ha!' He made a pretence of mopping his brow. 'Ye gods!' He fell into a deep armchair opposite Captain Maestrangelo. The Marshal stood at the window, his large, black uniformed shoulders blocking most of the light, staring out in silence. Fara was out there in the courtyard, in his usual place in the car. Given the presence of the Captain and the Prosecutor, there was nothing else for it. Directly below the window the sun was warming the polythene shrouds of the lemon trees, the uneven stones of the yard, the red roof of the little barn. For the almond tree it was too late. The tiny unfolding buds were dropping around it, their frail pink petals burnt brown by the bitter wind. Beyond the bare lines of the sloping vineyard lay an olive grove, its silvery leaves pale against the glossy brown folds of a ploughed field. Far below, the city of Florence spread its terracotta roofs and marble towers against a backcloth of blue hills. Even after all these years, the Marshal never tired of looking at it. At this distance, filthy pavements, unemptied rubbish skips, traffic jams and the stink of drains and exhaust fumes ceased to exist. At this distance it was a paradise and the gentle warmth of the sun and the quietness lay over everything like a blessing. Except for the almond tree . . . 'This is the fax from her lawyer's office—that's your copy, Maestrangelo—and there should be one with a translation attached for Guarnaccia who seems to be admiring the view . . .'

Trees . . . a country lane . . . Vittorio. Still, the memory wouldn't surface, at least not as far as his brain. It surfaced as far as his stomach, bringing a feeling of fear and nausea that he repressed. Clearly he didn't want to remember and yet Forbes was provoking him to it. It was absurd! What connection could there possibly be . . . ?

'It's a sizeable amount of money and, of course, there are other considerations, the chief of them being that she was intending to leave him and from what I've seen of Forbes . . . Can I offer you a cigar?'

'No, thank you.'

'Hope they don't bother you. Now this Forbes character . . . There was a paternity suit but the girl's parents refused to let her marry him. Payments are being made by Forbes's parents but they want nothing further to do with him and it suits them that Celia Carter took him off to Italy. That all sounds in character, I'd say.'

What if it wasn't a connection that had to do with facts, but only with feelings? Because he had to admit, though he was reluctant to do it, that a similar feeling of fear and nausea had been building up inside him for some time, and that he was trying to smother it, trying not to acknowledge its meaning, just as he tried not to acknowledge the memory of Vittorio, trees, a country lane. How long had he been feeling like that? He couldn't pinpoint it. After he'd talked to Father Jameson, perhaps . . .

A fit of coughing interrupted his thoughts. He was enveloped in a cloud of Fusarri's cigar smoke.

'All right, Guarnaccia, point taken. I'll try and hold out without my cigar for ten minutes. Open the window, if you like—I'm sure Eugenia won't mind—and then, for goodness' sake come and sit down.'

The Marshal did as he was told. He opened the window. The noise disturbed a small bird which darted out of the vine covering the wall of the house and flew away chattering angrily. Then the Marshal remembered.

'My feeling is that once we've got our thoughts in order we should go over there and face him with it. A confession's our only hope, obviously, unless somebody has a brainwave about how he did it. What about it, Guarnaccia?'

Getting no response, Fusarri looked inquiringly at the Captain who, more than a little irritated, called his Marshal to order. 'I don't think we're getting your full attention on this. Guarnaccia—Guarnaccia, are you feeling all right?'

'Yes, sir.'

'Good. Now I'd like to be a bit surer of my ground here and what isn't clear is his current behaviour, all this drawing attention to himself, these bizarre episodes—I take it we can rely absolutely on Signora Torrini's account of today's events?'

'Ah! Dear Eugenia!' Forgetting his promise, Fusarri lit up and blue clouds issued forth again. 'Yes, well, I'd say you can rely on her telling the truth and nothing but the truth, but not necessarily the whole truth, if you see what I mean.'

'I'm not sure that I do.' The Captain wasn't surprised that Guarnaccia couldn't cope with this sort of thing. He'd forgotten himself how difficult it was.

'What I'm trying to say is that dear Eugenia wouldn't tell a lie. If she says there was a violent quarrel over there at the barn and that she was seriously afraid the daughter might meet a similar fate to her mother's, then she certainly meant it. And if she says that Forbes then came over here and tried to buy the Villa Torrini, frightening her to death in the process, then I'm sure that's what happened. All I'm saying is that she's elderly and very upset, and that there are things she will have failed to notice or forgotten to mention in the telling of it, and we must allow for that.'

'Yes, of course. Well the best thing would be for one of us to go over it again with her tomorrow when she's had a little time to calm down—you don't think her son ought to come and stay with her?'

'Giorgio? Hm. He'd come if I insisted and leave after the first half-hour or the first quarrel whichever was the sooner. Better leave Giorgio out of this. He's still furious with her about the priest—Guarnaccia, are you sure you're all right?'

'Yes, the priest . . .' Shocked out of his reverie, he automatically repeated the Prosecutor's last words the way the teacher used to make him do at school, because at school was where he was in his head.

'The priest . . . yes, she did say that first night I came here that she'd called the priest and that Giorgio was furious. But there was no priest here so I never quite . . .'

'There you are, that's precisely what I'm telling you!' Fusarri smiled bright-eyed at the two of them. 'She called the priest all right but that was months ago. She called him to stop him ringing his blasted bells—and I quote—at six in the morning and waking her up when she often only got to sleep at three, being an insomniac. She told him his parishioners had alarm clocks and if they were foolish enough to go to mass at all, let alone at six in the morning, they could damn well set them. I gather from Giorgio who went round to the church to apologize, that he needn't have bothered since she forgot to announce herself, just said her piece and rang off. The amazing thing is that the unfortunate priest, young and full of missionary zeal, then called her to apologize, in the hope of coming round and bringing her back into the fold. He was saved from an unpleasant interview by the fact that she only answers the phone at one o'clock when Giorgio checks in to see if he's still a martyred son or a newly orphaned heir. Anyway, since he hasn't forgiven her and it's still a bone of contention, she mixed it in with the Celia Carter business as if it had just happened. That's what we have to guard against.'

Poor Signora Torrini had indeed been terrified, not so much by the row, and the sight of young Jenny fleeing the barn in hysterics, as by Forbes's attempt on her house. Having endured his good deeds against her will so often in the past, she was far from convinced that his offer to take the place off her hands at a generous price wouldn't come about whether she wished it or not. This time she had called the Marshal and then 'dear Virgilio' for good measure. The Marshal himself had asked the Captain to be present, telling himself that he'd soon need to ask him for at least one extra man. Telling himself a good many very logical things other than the truth, which was his need to have the Captain by him because of a growing sense of foreboding which had something to do with a memory he would rather keep repressed.

Well, now it was out. He had sat down because somebody had told him to, but he got to his feet again now with a sigh. His slightly bulging eyes strayed again to the window.

'Wait here,' he said, since he had to do this alone.

He didn't notice the Captain making to follow him, his face red with annoyance, or Fusarri's delighted grin and restraining gesture. Nor, seeing Fara down there in the car, did he register that he hadn't left him waiting upstairs. As he hammered on Sissi's door he was oblivious of those who watched him. Maestrangelo and Fusarri from the open window to his left, Fara from the car, Forbes from behind the lattice-work of the barn.

Only Sissi, opening the door to him, understood.

She wasn't smiling. She followed him as he walked past her, her little eyes watchful.

'Couldn't it wait a day? She's in a bad way just now.'

'Where is she?'

'The bedroom. There. We understand each other, she and I.'

'Yes.'

'Should have got out. Only answer. I used to dream of some terrible accident, my mother's face scarred for ever so I'd feel sorry for her. Look after her. One good thing about old age. I'd be ugly now anyway. Ha! Families. You don't think I should stay?'

'No.'

'Shan't listen. Don't want to. It's a bad business. Look at me: I haven't cried since I was seventeen. That's what people do to you. Better without.'

The Marshal knocked on the bedroom door and went in, closing it behind him.

CHAPTER 10

She hadn't heard him. She was asleep. She lay facing him on a rumpled quilt, her forearms crossed protectively over her chest, her knees drawn up, trails of waving blonde hair covering the pillow beneath her creased, tear-stained cheek and clinging to the black wool of her sweater.

Still, his entrance must have disturbed her troubled sleep because she turned with a deep shuddering sigh and stretched out on her back, her arms still crossed over her breast. She muttered a few words which the Marshal couldn't catch and then lay immobile. In that position she might have been an effigy on some mediæval tomb such as the Marshal had so often seen. But no knight in repose lay beside her, his last battle fought, his pointed toes turned hopefully towards heaven. And where else could you turn, when it came down to it? Who else could be called to comfort her, in the moment of the Marshal's distress, if not a Father Jameson? He thought of Mary Mancini, but she was Celia's friend. You needed someone who could go beyond that, someone who could pity the girl a little, and blame her mother a little for too much love.

His own mother, now . . . He was in his forties and it had taken all these years and *this* for him to begin to appreciate her ability to cope, to comfort. Half her attention on the weekly wash, reducing tragedy to the level of the missing button, the poor-yielding cow, the crying child. Deal with it and carry on. That's life and the rest is death, the only incurable evil. If he'd appreciated her then he would have told her all of it, not the censored version. Of course, thinking back now, she might have guessed it all and kept her counsel. Knowing him as she did, how could she have believed he'd wept in distress just because of the disturbed bird's nest? But that was what he'd told her.

'We climbed up, and Vittorio . . . and Vittorio . . . he touched one of the eggs—but why did the bird fly away like that? Why didn't it stay and peck him? Why didn't it peck his eyes out? Why? It just flew away as far as it could, singing and swooping about! It was stupid! It should have pecked his eyes out and made him fall out of the tree!'

And she had dried his tears and asked no questions. She must have known. How could she not have known that a boy, even at his tender age, didn't cry because some bird had flown its nest and sung its heart out to no avail. She had washed his scraped legs and told him that the mother bird had been trying to distract them, that in her ignorance, her wild behaviour was designed to take their attention from what she didn't want them to see.

But Vittorio, laughing, had turned back and looked down at him and, laughing and laughing, stuffed the birds' eggs into his mouth and crunched.

'They're not eggs! There are birds inside! You can't!'

He had dropped down, barking his shins, taken to his heels and run, but the image of those hairless little embryos crunched between Vittorio's bloody teeth followed him until he vomited in the dusty yellow road, and he couldn't hate Vittorio because Vittorio was hungry and had asked him for his snack, but his mother had told him not to give it, so he couldn't confess . . .

But only the female offers its life for its offspring. Perhaps that simple fact of nature had delayed him so long as he watched the elaborate gyrations of Julian Forbes, trying to attract his attention to false vices. He had only been trying to protect himself, to keep the Marshal distracted from the one truth that pointed to his guilt, the one woman, if such he could call her, who had not refused him, who had reasons of her own for accepting him, and who now knew she'd been used in her turn. Now there was no one to forgive her. Celia Carter, grieved beyond human endurance at her betrayal by the only two people in the world she had loved without question, had forgiven her, but she was dead.

The Marshal would have given a lot to believe that the tears drying streakily on Jenny Carter's fair cheeks were tears of grief for her mother but he knew in his heart they were for herself, and that was the saddest thought of all. He roused himself to face it and spoke:

'Signorina!'

She opened her eyes but they were drugged with sleep and didn't, at first, register his presence.

'We have to talk.'

She saw him then, but without surprise, as though he'd been there when she'd cried herself to sleep. She sat up and let her stockinged feet drop over the side of the bed.

'What time is it?'

'Ten to six.'

'She told you, didn't she? Sissi told you . . .'

'No, no . . . She didn't tell me.'

'But you know?'

'Yes.'

All trace of that rigid composure of their last meeting had gone. Her face was blotched and creased with crying and her shoulders sagged forward under their burden of hair.

'I'm so miserable. I wish I were dead instead of her . . .'

'That's no way to talk when you've your whole life in front of you.'

'What life? Where am I supposed to go? What am I supposed to do! I've got nobody!' She broke into fresh tears but made no attempt to cover her face. Saliva trickled from her mouth to mingle with the fast rolling tears. Her nose was running. The Marshal offered her a folded white handkerchief but she whipped her face away angrily.

'What am I supposed to do! He doesn't give a sod about me!'

The Marshal sat down on a round-backed chair with a nightdress and underwear thrown upon it.

'You've known that for a long time, now, haven't you? He must have broken it off before Christmas when he tried to stop you coming over for the holidays. Isn't that true?'

'Only because he was scared of her finding out! Only because she had all the money, because she—'

'No, no . . . And what about the others?'

'What others?' Her swollen eyes flashed into jealous life.

'Didn't you know that, in his rage at his feeling so inferior to your mother, he tried to go to bed with each of her women friends in turn?'

'I don't believe you.'

'Ask them. They refused him, of course. They thought a great deal of your mother. Then, presumably, he decided to try you. Something of hers he could take, a lesser version of her he could control. When did it start?'

She didn't answer him at once, as though still taking in what she'd just heard. Her hands were curling into tightly clenched fists on her knees and her breathing was uneven.

'I'll kill him . . .'

'Why? Didn't you have the same idea? To steal something that was hers? You could have had any number of boyfriends of your own. When did it start?'

'I was still at school.' She didn't look him in the face.

Horrified though he felt by this girl's behaviour, the Marshal, too, felt murderous about Forbes. After all, she had been only a schoolgirl.

'I suppose he helped you with your exams?'

She nodded.

'But you couldn't have seen much of each other once you were at university and they were living out here.'

'He used to come to London. He was supposed to be

trying to get journalistic commissions, stuff like that. We stayed in the house there.'

'In your mother's house. And when you came here?'

'She was out a lot doing her own things, research for books and stuff like that.'

Stuff that fed, housed and clothed them, while they . . .

'I wanted to tell her, then we could have gone away together.'

'Living on what?'

She shrugged. 'We'd have managed.'

'But he wouldn't?'

'No . . .' Her face collapsed in misery. 'I thought he was bored with me because I wasn't as clever or as interesting as her. Then when I came they made me sleep here! Nobody cares about me! Nobody! Why don't you arrest him? He killed her! He killed her in the end to get me!'

'No . . .' The Marshal hardly dared breathe. If she insisted on lying, her evidence against Forbes would be less than useless, a hysterical accusation that would be thrown out of court in minutes. He had to make her tell the truth but he didn't know how.

'This man,' he began gently, 'has already taken from you your mother who loved you, your peace of mind, your youth. If he gets away with what he's done he will also take a large amount of money which should be yours and which came originally from your father. Do you remember your father?'

'I . . . yes . . .' That seemed to quieten her.

'He provided for you, through your mother. Both of them loved you. Forbes told your mother what had happened between you when he'd decided which side his bread was buttered on and wanted to be rid of you. If you want to know how much your mother suffered because of it, go and talk to a priest called Father Jameson.'

'She never went to church.'

'No. But, you see, she was desperate and there was no one she could tell. She was ashamed.'

'Of me?'

'Perhaps. I think of herself, of admitting that the two people she practically worshipped hated her and were making a fool of her. In any case, she told no one except this priest, a stranger, and so she preserved your reputation.'

'What's the difference, now? You know.'

'Yes. I know. But there's no reason why anyone else should. Forbes killed your mother because she had announced that she intended to leave him. Her lawyers will confirm that because she had made an appointment to see them about it. She didn't give a motive. There's no reason why anyone has to know.'

'What if *he* tells?' She wiped a hand over her wet face and this time accepted the white handkerchief.

'He can't afford to tell. It would double the seriousness of the case against him and ensure his being found guilty and getting a very much heavier sentence. No, he won't tell.'

She sat in silence for a moment, blew her nose and pushed back the strands of hair that clung to her wet face. Then she looked him straight in the eyes. 'In that case, how come you haven't arrested him?'

'For one very simple reason,' the Marshal said, 'I don't know how he did it.'

'Don't you?' The girl let out a bitter, disgusted laugh. 'Well, I know, nobody better. And he knows I do, and even when I told him so, he still wouldn't have me. Is it true what you said about him and my mother's friends?'

'Yes, it's true.'

'He attacked me when I said I'd tell.'

'We'll see that you're protected.'

'He never loved me, did he?'

'No.'

Then she told him.

'I don't want to tell Katy,' Mary Mancini said.

'No,' agreed the Marshal, 'don't tell her or anyone else. We don't intend to bring it in as evidence. It would go worse for him if we did, but the damage to the girl . . .'

'Yes. There's been enough damage done there. I suppose we ought to think she's young and will get over it, but I don't know . . .'

The Marshal, thinking of the almond tree, didn't know either.

They were in Mary's sunny kitchen again. Katy had taken Jenny to her room to unpack.

'They should leave for England as soon as you can arrange it.'

'That's no problem. They were meant to leave tomorrow, anyway. They've got tickets. Term starts the day after. Even so, are you sure she'll be safe?'

'Well, we'd prefer her not to return to the university. If you could help, if you know someone who'd have her just till this is over . . .'

'Of course. She can go to my mother's. It's a tiny seaside place and Forbes knows nothing about her. Katy could go to her at weekends—Oh dear . . .' Mary stopped and gazed out at the huge crown of the evergreen tree, peacefully still now, and shining in the winter sunshine.

'Do you know, when you told me—no, even while you were just beginning to tell me about Julian and Jenny . . . it was as if, underneath, I knew. As if I'd known all along. It was the only explanation of everything, wasn't it? But I lacked the courage or the honesty, or whatever was needed to think it.'

'I believe I was the same. I should have faced it sooner.'

'But just think of Celia . . . She lived with it. She knew

them both inside out and loved them both. Think how she must have suffered and for how long before he made her face it. How *could* he tell her! Can't you arrest him even now?'

'Not yet. We want the girl away, so it looks as though she has no evidence of interest for us. Then we have to wait.'

'But wait for what?'

In a sense, it was the same story. Once it had happened, the Marshal would be able to say that he knew exactly all along what he had been waiting for. In the meantime, he didn't even spend much time thinking about it, not consciously. He hadn't even gone along to talk to the pathologist who had snapped his fingers and cried delightedly, 'Brilliant! And a first for me!' Adding, in sober afterthought, 'I wouldn't bruit it about too much in the papers. A bit too easy for comfort, don't you think?'

This was recounted to him by the Prosecutor, Fusarri, in his smoke-filled office to which the Marshal had been summoned.

'Now tell me what you want to do?'

'Just follow him.'

'Covertly or overtly?'

'What . . . it doesn't matter . . .'

Fusarri parked his little cigar in the left-hand corner of his mouth, sat well back and picked up the phone.

'How many men?'

'Just two, if the Captain can spare a car . . . But I want Fara with them.'

'Fara?'

'He's—' the Marshal was sufficiently *compos mentis* not to say 'my driver'—'one of my men. He's taken notes throughout the case . . .'

As indeed he had. The Marshal had been astonished at the extent of them. Fara, red-faced, had explained that

Lorenzini had advised him that he should try and learn something.

'Fara knows the places Forbes frequents, his habits, his acquaintances. He'll be a help.'

At which point, the Marshal left and went about his everyday business and you'd need to know him as well as Brigadier Lorenzini knew him to realize that his jaw might as well have been locked on Julian Forbes's calf for all the chance that miserable man had of escaping him.

It took five days. Then Fara called him at a little after six in the morning.

Teresa, despite his grabbing the phone almost before it had completed one ring, sat up, wide awake.

'Salva! What's to do?'

'Nothing. I'm needed in the office.'

'At this time?'

'It's all right. Go back to sleep. Somebody's been arrested.'

'Well, why aren't they at Borgo Ognissanti? Why here? Salva?'

Which was also the Marshal's first question, whispered.

'Why is he here? You should have taken him to Headquarters!'

'We did, but both cells are full. He had to be on his own, didn't he? What else could we do?'

The Captain's two men were there in the waiting-room with Fara, one still swinging his handcuffs.

'Do you need us?'

'No, no . . . you can go.' The fewer people knew about this, the better. But when they opened the door to leave, Galli was standing there, about to press the bell.

Before the Marshal could protest, Fara said, 'He helped, it was at Il Caffè, so I said . . .'

'All right—no, the photographer, no.'

'And I've just got him out of bed.' The photographer

retreated down the stairs behind the Captain's men and
Galli came in. Fara locked the door behind him and Galli
shrugged the loden overcoat from his shoulders.

'I feel half dead . . .' Nevertheless, he was as sleek as
ever, not a hair out of place.

'Is he out cold?' Galli wandered to the cell door and
peeked in. 'God, what a stink. Did he talk?'

Fara looked unhappily at the Marshal who took Galli
aside, one heavy hand on his shoulder.

'Do me a favour, will you? Go home and stay there until I
call you. Then you can come back with your photographer.'

'But—'

'You said to me yourself the other day, there's no such
thing as a scoop. It'll be on tonight's news whatever you
do.'

'I have my own reasons—'

'I know. And I'm telling you, as I wouldn't tell anybody
else, that I can't do what I have to do if you're here.'

'You're up to something. Understood. I'll go.' On the
stairs he looked back up at the Marshal. 'Get him. Promise
me you'll get that bastard.'

'I will.' The Marshal closed and locked the door. He and
young Fara stood looking at each other. 'How long has he
been out cold?'

'About three hours. He started a fight in Il Caffè. Galli
helped, letting him hang around and seeing he got enough
drink down him, though it didn't take much before he got
aggressive, and then Galli really got him going. He'd seen
us outside.'

'But he knows nothing?'

'Oh no. He probably just thought we wanted an excuse
to pick him up. Either that or he had some private grudge
of his own. Anyway, it was a good help—oh, and I'd better
tell you, when we arrested him he snatched a flask of wine
from a table. I did take it off him when we put him in the

car, but between one thing and another he managed to get to drink most of it.'

'All right.'

'The other two don't know. It's just that he hadn't had enough, not to knock him out enough so he'll remember nothing. I threw the flask—'

'What flask? Go and make some coffee—where are the notes?

'On your desk, ready.'

'Then let's start waking him up . . .' He opened the flap to look at Forbes who lay on his back with his beard pointing at the ceiling of the tiny cell. A large blue bucket, thoughtfully placed beside him by Fara, was the source of the reek of vomit. Forbes was snoring loudly. 'If we can't waken him properly you can call a doctor. I want him in a fit state to be able to get a lawyer.'

Fara was reading aloud. He began tentatively, the presence of the Captain, the Prosecutor and Forbes's lawyer intimidating him. Forbes himself was so ill it was all he could do to remain upright in his chair, and you could see that he was afraid to make the slightest movement with his head in case he vomited again. His hands clutched the sides of the chair seat, the knuckles white. Fara continued, glancing every now and then at the Marshal, seeking a supportive nod or even a sympathetic expression. But the Marshal showed no expression at all. He might not have been listening.

He was listening, in his own way. He heard every word, took in every detail of the story. It was just that he wasn't hearing Fara's voice telling it. It was Jenny's voice we heard. A voice weary and hoarse with crying, emptied of emotion because even the most violent emotion succumbs to tiredness in the end.

'It was a game we had. He called it bathing the baby.

He used to soap me all over, even wash inside my ears and between my toes. Then, to rinse me, he'd take me by the ankles and swim me up and down making waves that swilled the soapsuds away. Mostly we did it in London, but sometimes we did it here as well when she was out. I don't think he's kinky, I mean about little girls. He just liked looking after me, being the strong one. I didn't mind. I'm not strong like my mother. I didn't feel guilty. Why should I? She had everything, she didn't need him as well. If I'd studied for the rest of my life I'd never have achieved anything compared to her. And she was always making a thing about being so careful not to make me feel it. When I started learning the piano, when we were still living in London, she stopped playing. Did she think I didn't know why? She might just as well have said I would never be as good as her and have done with it. Sometimes I hated her enough to kill her but that wasn't the reason. I was in love with him, whatever you think. He didn't make me feel stupid.

'One day there was this accident. We were in London. I was on half-term and he'd come over for an interview for some journalistic job. He didn't make that up, there really was an interview. He promised me if he got the job he'd leave her, that she could stay in Italy and we could get a flat in London. Only he didn't get the job. She ruined it for him. All his references were references she'd organized for him. The articles he'd sent in had been commissions of hers she'd dumped on him and then half written for him. He had no confidence at the interview because of all that. It made him feel guilty. He'd have got the job if it hadn't been for her. When I met him outside afterwards he was in a cold sweat. We went and had a drink and then a meal with some good wine to cheer him up. Julian said it served her right if we were spending her money, since it was her fault that it had gone wrong. Afterwards, we went back to the house. We were a bit drunk. Julian ran the bath and filled it very full with lots of perfumes and foam in it. That's when the accident happened. He was pulling me back and forth with my ankles and I was squealing, just in fun. Then he pulled too hard and the water came up over my face. There was so much foam and he didn't notice. He just kept pushing and pulling and there was water in my lungs and I couldn't get upright because he had my ankles. My head wasn't in the water but I couldn't breathe. It was only so that he could turn the cold shower on me for a joke that he let go. I tried to pull myself over the side of the bath but I lost consciousness. When I came round I was on the floor and he was trying to give me artificial respiration, pressing on my back, but he didn't really know how to do it. He was crying, he was so scared. I only thought after he'd gone back that what he was scared of was that if I'd died he'd have been in trouble, that he'd have been stuck there with my body and *she'd* have found out.

'When he got back here he rang me and said it all had to stop. He told me not to come out at Christmas. He confessed to her so that *she'd* stop me coming out at Christmas, and when she didn't he sold my bed.

'When I heard she was dead I knew what he'd done. I thought he'd done it for me. I thought he'd decided at last . . . but she had him on a string till the last, had him running round after her, taking her her drink in the bath! She had him begging her! Begging her not to leave him but she wouldn't give in. She didn't give a damn for him. He was just trying to make her listen to him. He didn't do it for me, he just wanted her to stay with him, and so he pulled and pulled and he didn't let go! He could see from her eyes she was terrified but she didn't give in, so he held on. She dropped her glass and tried to get hold of the side of the bath, like I did, but he just held her heels higher. It was so easy. When he let go she slid into the water on the broken glass and the water went pink. He's frightened of blood. He went to the bedroom to have a drink because of the blood. He wasn't upset about her. Whatever you say, you don't know him, he didn't love her. She'll still try to hold on to him, won't she? Even now she's dead. But now I've got money. I can get him a good lawyer. You can arrest him, now I've told you, and then I'll pay for the lawyer. He'll owe me that.'

Because of the blood. After that I can't remember.

Fara's account had lost synchronization with the Marshal's mental processes. But then, it was shorter. There were things they hadn't written. Forbes looked no more nor less ill than he had when they'd started. He was beyond caring. The lawyer, on the other hand, was looking as though he'd rather not have been called to such a hopeless case.

'Has my client signed this so-called confession?'

'No, no . . .' the Marshal said with equanimity. 'We're not even considering it as such, given the state he was in when we brought him here . . . particularly—' he looked hard at the lawyer—'particularly because of the involvement of a young girl who, having already lost her mother . . .'

He gave it three days. Within that time, the Marshal felt, a suitable confession to the murder of Celia Carter, excluding all damning references to her daughter, would have been signed.

He was wrong. It took only two days. But then, as the Marshal confessed to Galli in the bar across from Borgo Ognissanti, 'I'm a bit on the slow side myself, so . . .'

'You got him. That's all that matters—and Mary Mancini will probably be Celia's literary executor, had you heard?'

'No. I didn't know.'

'Can I offer you another?'

'No, no . . . There's something I have to see to.'

'Is that all?' Signora Giorgetti wiped her soapy hands on her apron and looked at the black plastic sack the Marshal was bringing into the kitchen.

'It's just the little girl's clothes and toys, or what I could find of them. The magistrate made an exception. He'll have to sign an order releasing the rest—'

The old woman sank down on a kitchen chair and wept.

'I spent every penny I had—*and* got myself into debt—trying to keep her flat for her. What did they want putting her in prison? They had that brute Saverino and poor Antonio, what did they have to take my daughter for?'

'Now, now.' A neighbour, who had probably been camping there all morning, stood up and got hold of the old woman's shoulders. 'Don't take on. You've the child to think of.'

'She should never have left Antonio! None of this would have happened if she hadn't left Antonio!'

'Don't take on, now! D'you hear what I say?' The neighbour gave the Marshal a despairing glance and lit a cigarette. The ashtray in the middle of the plastic-covered table was already overflowing.

The old woman blew her nose loudly and then yelled, 'Fiammetta!'

The child came in. She was wearing her pink tracksuit and dirty white trainers.

'I've brought your toys,' the Marshal offered, holding the open mouth of the plastic sack towards her. She didn't move.

'Have you brought Gobbly Bear?'

'I—I brought everything I could find . . .'

The child shot forward and grabbed at the sack, emptying its contents out on to the floor.

'Fiammetta!' Her grandmother aimed a whack at her but missed. The little girl ignored her, shaking, kicking and stamping at the jumble of clothing, shoes and toys at her feet. Then, breathing heavily but not crying, she retreated until her back was against the wall and began sucking fiercely on her thumb.

'Can't you see your gran's upset?' admonished the neighbour. 'What sort of behaviour's that? You say thank-you to the Marshal for bringing your toys!' She got up and stubbed out her cigarette. 'I'm off. You can leave her with me after if you need to.'

When the two women were at the door, murmuring, the Marshal looked at Fiammetta and said, 'I'm sorry. Are you sure you left him there? I didn't see a bear.'

Fiammetta stared, sucking her thumb and banging her thin little back rhythmically against the wall.

Her grandmother came back and started picking up the stuff from the floor and putting it back in the sack.

'Take no notice. It's nothing. Just a drawing her dad did for her. It was stuck on the wall over the bed. She's toys enough here.'

'I'm sorry.'

Fiammetta sucked and rocked, staring out at him from her withered young face. The kitchen was small and oppressive. The Marshal felt the need to get out in the street and breathe some air.

It didn't bring him much relief. The city had been a week, now, without wind. Via Mazzetta was blocked solid by a queue of cars. They and the people coming towards the Marshal were colourless silhouettes against a foggy glare.

'Ouff!' He fished out his sunglasses. Now there'd be a pollution warning and tomorrow there'd be a traffic ban, and tomorrow . . . a ritual battle with no victory even hoped for.

The Marshal trudged along slowly, trying not to inhale the fumes too deeply.

From behind closed windows came the muffled signature tune of the lunch-time news. Metal shutters started rattling down over shop windows and a brief waft of meat sauce, heavy with garlic and rosemary, reached his nostrils.

A dusty workman with a brown paper bag protecting his head hurried past the Marshal, whistling, with a kilo of bread under one arm and a flask of red under the other.

The Marshal, too, quickened his pace.